About the Author

Chris Munro lives in a small town in Ontario, Canada, working as a butcher and playing far too much dungeons and dragons. He started telling stories at a young age which slowly grew into a passion for writing.

No Signal at Whitman Station

Chris Munro

No Signal at Whitman Station

Olympia Publishers
London

www.olympiapublishers.com
OLYMPIA PAPERBACK EDITION

Copyright © Chris Munro 2023

The right of Chris Munro to be identified as author of
this work has been asserted in accordance with sections 77 and 78 of
the Copyright, Designs and Patents Act 1988.

A CIP catalogue record for this title is
available from the British Library.

ISBN: 978-1-80439-191-4

This is a work of fiction.
Names, characters, places and incidents originate from the writer's
imagination. Any resemblance to actual persons, living or dead, is
purely coincidental.

First Published in 2023

Olympia Publishers
Tallis House
2 Tallis Street
London
EC4Y 0AB

Printed in Great Britain

Dedication

To Nick, Lucas and Jordan. Thanks for the inspiration.

Acknowledgements

Thanks to my good friend, Nick and my sister, Shawna for encouraging me.

Prologue

In the year 2347, the human race has reached forth and claimed many systems of the Milky Way through sheer determination and human intuition. Prosperity flourished as planets, moons and even several asteroids were slowly stabilized and terraformed to be hospitable for human life. Just as they were on the brink of a second golden age of space fairing and colonization, a rebellion broke out that left Earth and all its colonies stranded in the depths of a depression. As Earthling High Command and the military focused on regaining control of the Sol solar system, it left many other outlying systems to fend for themselves until the heart of the civilization could be restored and focus could then be turned to its appendages. The war ended eight years ago, and though the far colonies were not completely abandoned by Earth, they still must rely upon themselves to survive.

Chapter 1

Nothing Ever Changes

My head rings as the morning alarm blares through the speakers of the officer's wing, pulling me from my slumber. *"Morning protocol has begun, please commence daily procedures,"* the station's prerecorded PA system slurs out through crackling speakers. I sit up with a slow stretch and groan and stare at my room's thick steel solar blinds as they activate with a soft click and open then fold into the walls, letting the bright sun fill the room in an instant with its never-ending daylight. I stand slowly with aches in my body and make for the sink and splash my face with cold water. *"Why the hell did I take this position?"* I stare at my aging face and think to myself for the first time today, knowing it will cross my mind another twenty times before lunch. I relieve myself and activate the glass door to my steam shower; stepping in I know these are the few minutes I will get alone and off camera today. I sit on the white porcelain tile floor with my chin on my knees. *'Fuck, my arms hurt.'* I mumble to myself as my fingers run slowly over the Cervo implants on my neck and shoulders. I know I need to work out more but my position hasn't allowed me much time for it as of late. My mind wanders as I sit in the thick steam. I see myself back on the planet Arili, wearing my C-suit with my squad. Giving orders and leading the charge, back when that meant something. Here I'm just a shulb, in charge of what are practically children, dealing with person-to-person drama as opposed to the tactical combat I used to coordinate. As my old glory passes before my mind's eye and fade into a brief moment of peace, a crackling sound followed by a ping erupts in my room over the speakers and snaps me back to reality.

"Commander Haves, sorry to disturb you, sir, but you have an appointment with Doctor Vyers in twenty minutes," Lieutenant Toric announces through the PA system.

I silently wretch at the idea of yet another realignment of my shoulders, knowing it is what Dr. Vyers will request. I sigh and slide the glass steam door open and grab my haptic glove from on top of the toilet and press the comms button.

"Copy that, central. Inform Dr. Vyers that I am Oscar Mike." A low buzz of quiet static hums before I hear a reply.

"Uhh. Oscar Mike, sir?" he replies with a questioning tone.

"I am on the move, Toric; Oscar Mike means on the move," I say bluntly and sigh as I roll my eyes. *'My god, the kid's an idiot,'* I think to myself as I stand and shake my head at the ineptitude of these rookie soldiers. Hell, I shouldn't even call them soldiers, this recon station has more maintenance crew than combat-ready veterans.

"Of course, yes, copy that, sir. I'll inform Dr. Vyers," he says with clear embarrassment on his voice as the comm link to the speakers ends with another ping and I step from the steam shower with a groaning stretch and dry myself, preparing for yet another day in this paradise.

I suit up in my grey and blue officer's uniform and slide my hand into my haptic utility glove, taking a brief moment to ensure my room is all in place. *'Bed, check. Shower, check. Shave, shit.'* I curse under my breath knowing I don't have the time now to remove my stubble. As I leave my room and walk the empty halls of the officer's wing, I run my hand down my cheeks to my chin hating the feel of the coarse greying hairs I find as my fingers trickle down. I am only one of three officers here on Whitman Station; Major Thorne leads my small contingent of twenty battle-ready Cervo-soldiers, and Major Pirez leads my engineering crew of just over two hundred men and women dedicated to our mission.

Whitman Station is a long-range sensory array and orbital defense station located in the far reaches of the Epsilon Eridani system, about ten light years from Earth. Built over forty years ago on a small terraformed moon known as P4X-1711, its original purpose was to be a surface port and habitat for those looking to claim a stake in the new expansion of the human race and its place in the galaxy. The journey to new locations across the systems quickly took a likeness to the old Oregon Trail of the long dissolved United States, and with that P4X-1711 took on the name Whitman Station. When the bloody *Serf War* broke out, the station was transformed into the defensive station we see today, equipped with a battery of two hundred and five rail guns built for surface-to-orbit combat along with an anti-air ionized rail-cannon. The moon itself is roughly two times smaller than that of Earth's moon, but similar in some ways as it is in a fixed orbit and does not spin. The lack of rotation gives us the advantage of consistent readings to our long-range scanners and low atmospheric central optics, although it causes the station to suffer from never-ending daylight as it orbits the Jupiter-like gas giant *Tau*.

I walk the solid steel walls of the barracks wing towards the medical center. As I slowly make my way past a long set of lockers, I see one of the doors has been left open. Looking closer as I pass, I see old graffiti scratched into the inner face of it stating

Scud Was Here, but the *Here* has been scratched out and beside it someone has carved *A Dud.* I shake my head with disappointment as I remember Corporal Scudinski and his incident with the ionized rail cannon. "That boy certainly was a dud," I whisper to myself as I turn the corner and enter the medical wing, its eggshell white halls reflecting the bright sunrays from its long line of picture windows that look down into the practice yards. My eyes squint as I look out into the yard and see Major Thorne suited up and running drills with the *Herd* as we call them, being that the Cervo-suit looks much like a two-legged half man, half deer with its antlers flared and slicked back, each about a foot long. I see him order commands and the troops follow flawlessly. He's young, only thirty-two, but he has the respect and loyalty of the Herd which is why I picked him for the position. I turn right just as I see the soldiers gearing up for a charge with their massive hoof-like magnetic boots – using small magnetic shockwaves it allows the user to burst forward with great leaps and immense speed, also giving them the ability to lock themselves in place if the need arises, making them perfect in zero-gravity combat.

I turn once again and see the door to Dr. Vyers' office at the end of the hall. I begin to breathe quickly and grow anxious as I activate the sliding door and enter the artificially lit medical room. My nose tickles at the heavy smell of disinfectant in the air. Along the left wall I see her three small medical droids power up and spring to life as they hover slowly in my direction; they dance around me in a floating ballet and begin performing preliminary scans. I walk to the solid steel observation table and sit as they follow and scan my face, chest and specifically my upper back and arms. I watch as they hum and beep, washing me in soft green light as they scan me from their main central eye protruding from a round disk-like green chrome shell, very similar to a turtle with no legs or tail.

I sit quietly for several minutes – only the humming of the droids and occasional beep or ping from the surrounding medical equipment breaks the silence – until from behind me a door slides open followed by the sound of soft footsteps. I turn my head slightly and peer over my shoulder to see the old but still very lively figure of Dr. Vyers in her lab coat. Her greying copper hair blocks her face as she is face down reading my scans and vitals from the holo-tab in her hands. Without looking up she drifts over to me and speaks in an almost robotic voice.

"You haven't been doing your exercises, Commander. If you remain inert, your implants will surrender to your artificial bones and you will lose function in both of them," she says in a blunt tone of disappointment and pulls a small metal rod and begins prodding at the cervo implants attached to each joint and every disk of my spine and shoulders, applying a small electric shock to each of them and checking their stats on her holo-tab as she does.

"I understand that, Doctor, but with the yearly reset and upload coming, my duties have taken lead over exercise," I say, trying to justify my reluctance to work out more as her prodding sends tingles through my spine in small waves.

"Duties are important, sir, but without your arms you will be discharged for negligence in the eyes of High Command. I'm very sorry, Commander, but I will have to add this to my report," she states as she finally looks up from her holo-tab, her eyes instantly locking on my jaw. "Hm, you should keep the beard, it suits you, sir," she says out of turn in a slightly less robotic voice.

I cringe at the notion and run my hands along the coarse hairs. "A simple misstep in morning protocol, that's all. I have a lot on my mind with the shut-down coming. Speaking of which, have you ensured all important files have been sent off to the central hub on Laramie?" I ask, pointing at her holo-tab.

"Sent off three days ago, sir. As you can see, I keep good order here in the medical wing," she quips as she smirks and motions to her three droids that do essentially eighty percent of her work. I roll my eyes as she knows she is one of the few people that can get away with such a sarcastic disregard for command. "Now I'll need you to assume the position and bite down on this," she says, offering me a small wooden dowel.

I lay forward on my stomach and bite down as I let my mind wander to my happy place back on Arili, my squad behind me as we take the fight to the *Serfs*. Twenty years ago, a small chain of newly habitable planets rose up against the other Earth-loyal planets, declaring independence for themselves and any others that wished to be free from what they called *Earthling tyranny*. Of course, the Earth loyalists took up arms against them and a twelve-year war ensued, which in the end left several dozen planets no longer habitable and caused the death of over nine billion innocent people. I was active for ten years of that war, stationed on the planet Arili – it was a highly fought-over planet due to its availability of high-quality iron deposits and massive foundries. I went from Private to Major in that time and was given charge of my own regiment. Our job was to protect locals and ensure the foundries stayed active. The Cervos were the heavy metal fist of that war and it couldn't have been won without them; their speed and strength gave us a heavy advantage against the serfs. I try to dwell more on my time on Arili but the pain of the realignment pulls me out as I scream and chew deep ridges into the dowel. The pain is excruciating to say the least.

Chapter 2

Officer on Deck

The realignment was as painful as usual, similar to cracking your knuckles but instead it's every artificial bone inside my torso. Ten years ago, an incident on Arili caused the breakage of a majority of the bones in my upper torso, forcing me to sit out the final years of the war in a hospital bed. Though my heroic actions came with heavy decoration from High Command, it left my body struggling against the artificial implants and the constant pain and realignments that go with it. *'I would do it all again if I had to,'* I think to myself as I walk the bright halls stiff as a board towards the command center.

I pass soldiers and crew coming from the first floor as they head for their daily routines, each of them giving a morning salute as they move to let me pass. As each one meets my gaze, I'm reminded of the great diversity our civilization has achieved and how far we have come as a people, each soldier and engineer coming from different reaches of our galaxy. Whitman Station is located far into the end of our habitable territory, approximately forty-seven billion kilometers from the nearest station, and was the second to last built along the Oregon Trail before the Serf War began and the final stages of the project were abandoned. The last station being *The Dalles*, which serves as a research and monitoring station for several planets currently being terraformed in our sector. Their bi-monthly fuel shipments which make their last stop here is the most activity we see, that and the rare smuggler or pirate raid, which in my eight years in command of this station, I have only seen five of and one prime shot from the rail guns usually does them in.

I continue my march as I pass technicians working to prepare the wall set holo-tab terminals for the upload, their fingers working the screens with fierce precision. I hear cheers as I come to an intersection not far from the entrance to the command center. Stepping forward and looking to my right I see five engineers cheering as two of them carry a keg. *'Are you fucking kidding me?'* I think as my jaw clenches and my gaze meets the eye of every engineer.

"Attention!" I yell as they jump, startled into a salute, the keg smacking the ground with a heavy thud. "Has the upload procedure begun?" I question with an intense tone.

"No, sir!" they all shout as a blush of red coats each of their faces, their eyes darting in embarrassment towards a few technicians that happened to be walking by.

"Have I given the *All-Clear* command?" I ask with a sarcastic tone, taking time to look each and every one in the eyes.

"No, sir!" they all shout again in unison, fear and embarrassment clear on their voices.

"Did all five of you have plans for the off-time during the upload today?" I question but none answer as they try to avoid my gaze. "Well?" I ask again with fading patience.

"We do, sir," Corporal Girard says in her usual meek voice.

"That's right," I say with a brief smile and look to each of them. "You've got maintenance duty with Major Pirez. I'll inform her that you are on your way." I nod with a forceful tone. "Dismissed," I bark as I stand and watch them until they round the corner. "You two," I point to two passing soldiers as they turn and salute, "take that keg to the cervo workshop and tell them it was a gift from engineering." They both nod with affirmatives and together grab the keg and walk down towards the first-floor atrium stairs as I make for the command center. *'Kids are gonna be kids if you don't watch them,'* I remind myself as I toggle the access panel to the bustling command center.

"Officer on deck!" Corporal Baron shouts almost directly into my ear as I walk in, seeing all fifteen technicians stand at attention; most are young barely twenty-five.

"At ease, staff," I say with my usual bravado. As they return to their duties, I walk to Lieutenant Toric's terminal station and loom over him for a brief moment. "Lieutenant Toric," I say loud enough to gather everybody's attention. "When addressing an officer through the comm system, I would prefer that you knew what you were doing." I throw a booklet down on his desk beside him. "Here is the beginners handbook issued to you at orientation. Reread it from cover to cover and memorize every code. Until then, you are relieved of comm-link duty." He shudders as I speak to him. He's a kid, easily no older than twenty.

"Yes, sir! Understood, sir!" he says boldly but a clear mask of embarrassment washes over his face as he grabs the booklet and opens it to the first page.

"Good, see to it," I say as I walk to my terminal station that overlooks everyone at their stations. I log in and view all open reports: three requests for vacation leave *'Approved'*, four maintenance tickets, and an injury report. After checking the notifications I pull up the itinerary for this year's upload procedure sent to us from *Laramie Station*. Once a year our outdated systems require an update from the command hub on Laramie, a space station about half way between here and the Sol solar system where Earthling High Command resides. Laramie is a massive space port built into an asteroid. It's placed in a fixed position by thruster rockets and houses a standing fighter force of over one thousand ships. It's not only responsible for the resource distribution of the Epsilon Eridani system, but also four other systems within the sector. There are two stations between Whitman and Laramie that the upload signal is bounced off of, *The Rock* and *Boise station.* The upload takes roughly ten hours and will cut off our external communications and long-range sensors for the duration. I finalize my preliminary check list and call to my second in command of the control center, Lieutenant Donovan. "Donovan, open the holo-link with Laramie Station and get Major York on the line."

"Connecting now, Commander," he says, looking up over his terminal as his fingers stride over its keyboard.

"Thank you," I say as I turn from my terminal and walk over to the station's holographic projector, which aside from the cervo units, is probably to most sophisticated piece of technology we have.

I stand in the shiny metallic circle on the floor as a small arm protrudes from the floor, the end of it flaring open with several scanners and cameras. I watch as it begins to whirl to life and rotate around me as it scans to create an image of me in the receiving circle of Laramie Station. As I stand and wait to connect with Laramie, I find my officer's posture hard to hold as my shoulders and arms scream in pain causing me to quiver slightly. I hold back, trying to hide the pain from my surrounding technicians. A few moments pass as a blue transparent figure begins to render in the receiving circle across from me. The figure is tall and clearly male, as the image clears and shows he is in a Commander's uniform. *'Not Commander Cairn, any day but today,'* I think to myself trying hard not to roll my eyes.

"Commander Haves, a pleasure as always." The figure salutes and smiles from behind a well-kept goatee and perfectly sculpted eyebrows.

"Commander Cairn, this is a surprise to say the least," I say with a hint of confusion. *'Something's wrong, I can just tell.'* I ponder at what the issue could be as he continues.

"Indeed, as I'm sure you were expecting Major York?" He asks inquisitively as he frowns and lowers his head in a brief moment of deep thought. "Bit of bad news, chap," he says, looking up and smiling, trying to lessen the blow of whatever bad news he has ready for me. "Seems Boise is having issues with high atmospheric sandstorms, and it has caused quite a mess of intermittent signal loss." He shrugs with a plain face knowing he isn't the one who has to deal with the issue.

"So the upload is cancelled? When will we reschedule to?" I ask briskly as this news will cause more than several complications.

"Unfortunately, High Command feels we should follow through and simply bounce the signal from The Rock." He shrugs again clearly holding back a smirk. *'Easy for you to say.'*

"That's ridiculous Cairn, that will easily double the upload period," I retort promptly with a flash of frustration.

"At minimum it will double it but orders are orders, Haves, you of all people should understand that, right? Or shall I call Admiral Granne and have the entire Eridani Armada change course to suit your needs?" he quips as the snide smile he has been holding back finally crosses his face. *'Dammit, if only you were here, you smug sonofabitch, I'd wipe that smile off your face.'*

"No need to bother the Admiral, I understand completely

Commander Cairn. Is that all? May we continue with our upload procedure?" I remark as I cross my arms out of anger but also to ease the weight on my shoulders.

"Proceed, Commander Haves," he says with sarcasm as he flicks his hand like a master ordering his servant around. Before he can do more I step from the metallic circle and cut the connection to the station. *'Limie bastard.'*

I breathe deeply and silently shake my head at the news I've just received and walk back to my terminal. All technicians turn their heads and return to their duties pretending they didn't just eavesdrop on the entire conversation. I stand in front of my bright terminal and exhale deeply as I activate a comms link to entire station.

"This is Commander Haves, may I have everyone's attention please," I order in my officer's tone and take another deep breath. "I have just been informed by Commander Cairn at Laramie station that there is interference on Boise and the signal will instead be uploaded solely from The Rock. This will likely double the length of the upload. Now, before you all start cheering, this does not mean you are excused from duty till then. Work assignments will be allocated once the upload has begun. More information will follow via your haptic gloves or any functioning terminals. Thank you." I close the link and sigh heavily. Within moments my comms light up with a link from Major Pirez down in engineering. "Pirez, status report," I order to her as my eyes dart across my terminal screen.

"Well, sir, to be honest, it would have been nice if they had told us sooner. I'm running new diagnostics now but it appears not much changes on our end except the timeframe." I can hear the rapid tapping on her keyboard as she makes any needed changes to the procedure. "We have a confirmed link with The

Rock now, sir, shall I begin the upload?" I can tell by her voice that she is anxious to get started. She enjoys the maintenance time during the shut-down and that time just doubled.

"First let's run through the checklist. What is the status on the gun belt?" I ask beginning my routines.

"One hundred and ninety-three fully operational, sir, thirteen down for maintenance and repairs. You'll see that I lumped them into four service tickets," she calls back almost instantly. I know she is ready but I still have to make my checks.

"I saw them, thank you. Status on the scanners?" I continue down the list of checks as I tick off each box.

"Local, short- and long-range scanners are all operational, sir," she recites with precision.

"Status on the ion cannon?" I ask with a slight wisp of humor.

She huffs as she answers with heavy sarcasm. "As you know, sir, since the *Scudinski incident* we've only been able to achieve eighty percent efficiency with thirty-seven shells available to fire, sir."

"Excellent," I say as I switch my comms to full crew frequency. "This is Commander Haves once again; I am issuing the order for everyone to log out of all terminals and power down your stations until the upload process has begun. This should take no more than three minutes. Thank you for your cooperation." I wait a minute and open a private link to Major Pirez. "All right Sasha, do your thing," I say with a slight hint of a smile on my face.

"With pleasure, sir," she says so gladly that I can hear the smile on her face through the speaker.

Within moments the entire station powers down and grows quiet, each system taking its turn to go quiet as terminals blink off one by one. A few minutes pass as everyone stands around quietly as the systems begin to return to life in a cacophony of beeps and buzzes. I log into my terminal as it regains power and see that both external communications and long-range scanners are down, which is exactly what I expected to see. I key my haptic comms to the Major. "Status check, Pirez."

"Everything appears to be operational; upload link is established and strong, readings say approximately twenty-three hours and some change before completion, sir," she says in a soft tone trying to lessen the blow of this ridiculous new timeframe.

"A whole day? That can't be right, Sasha," I ask with tempered confusion. *'Cairn said it would double it but I thought that might be an exaggeration.'*

"Sorry, Commander, the link is as strong as I can get it," she replies in a defensive tone. *'She would know best.'*

"This is going to be stressful but nonetheless you did an excellent job, Major; you may begin your maintenance routines," I say, confirming her checklist as my terminal glows with radiating blue light.

"Thank you, sir, beginning routines now," she says happily as her link ends. *'She may be the only person on this station that is happy about this.'*

"All right, crew," I say, opening another link to entire facility, "we have successfully linked with Laramie Station via The Rock and the upload should be completed in roughly one day. Again, this does not excuse anyone from their regular duties. Now, I'd like all nonessential personnel to please finalize your checklists and take your half day. Good work everyone and go enjoy your holiday," I finish and close the link as a majority of my technicians log out and begin to shuffle out of the command center. I double check everything and type a message to be auto-delivered to Laramie upon completion of the upload. I log out of my terminal and address Lieutenant Donovan.

"Donovan, the floor is yours. I'll be in my room if you require anything," I order as I step away from my terminal and make for the exit.

"Yes, sir, thank you, sir. I have everything under control; enjoy your downtime," he says, throwing up a well-practiced salute as I leave the command center though the right corridor.

Donovan is a smart kid; he's worked his way up from private under my command. He gladly accepted the Lieutenant's position when I offered it to him, against the wishes of his peers of course. The rank of Lieutenant is a grey area between an officer and a regular soldier, usually seen as the *kiss-ass* position by soldiers not fit for being officers. I myself see the position as a worthy title, as it shows one's commitment to our cause and oath as soldiers of Earth. Donovan shows much promise to be the station's next officer, and I can tell he wants it. His versatility is his greatest asset, a soldier one minute and a technician the next. His flawless transition of duties and ability to out-perform his peers has caught the eyes of both Majors Pirez and Thorne, both of whom support his grooming for the position of Major.

Chapter 3

"Precious" Memories

I traverse the halls towards the officer's wing passing dozens of personnel smiling with glee and chatting about their plans for their day off, most talk about drinking as it is the usual thing to do during the upload. Only one officer is allowed to be off duty during the upload and this year's rotation makes it my turn. A small smile crosses my lips as I contemplate my free day. Arriving in the quiet officer's wing I pass dozens of unoccupied rooms; with a full staff this wing alone could house a small army of officers. With the Serf War over this station has no need for such a large occupancy. We currently have just a little over enough to stay fully operational.

I key the code to my room on its exterior access panel and enter as the metal door slides into the ceiling. Upon entering I walk to the mirror and stand looking at myself. My brown eyes dance across my aging face, seeing the lines slowly digging deeper around my nose and across my forehead. My hand runs down my cheeks and as I feel the salt and pepper hairs scrape against my skin, I contemplate a shave but I think I'm growing fond of it. *'Maybe it'll grow on me,'* I think to myself with humor as I laugh to myself and turn away from the mirror.

I walk along my bookshelf, glancing at each title deciding which I should read today; all of them are history books on many different topics. I've always had a particular interest in man's fight for space; so far, we haven't seen any aliens, but we sure have found monsters within ourselves. I decide on a book about *Boudicca*, a Celtic queen born some twenty-four hundred years ago who rallied armies to her call after Rome took land she was to inherit. She defeated the Romans using guerilla war tactics but lost when they met the organized Roman ranks in an open field pitch battle.

Many serf war tactics were built around guerilla warfare used by humans for thousands of years; luckily my knowledge saved many lives when facing the serfs on Arili. They pulled many of their war tactics from *The Art of War* by Sun Tzu. They produced thousands of copies and distributed them amongst their ranks. In many ways it made warfare with them almost predictable as they followed word for word from the book. But for the smarter more ingenious serfs, it brought many innovations to their tactics. They would attack in far reaching places that took time to get to but would be gone when we arrived so they could assault elsewhere while we were preoccupied. They abandoned the teachings of the book about six years into the war due to High Command distributing their own counter measures to just about every passage in the book. The serfs then took to simply pillaging like savages and hiding in their strongholds for the remaining years of the war. As the rebel serf leaders were picked off, the war took a sick turn from there as the remaining rebels began killing innocent people as some sort of twisted revenge towards Earthling High Command.

I place the book on my desk and sit down looking up at my wall of trophies to distract myself from some of my more horrendous memories of war. Some are service awards but most were taken from serf strongholds and some claimed from space pirates. Maps, ancient and modern swords, archaic firearms, model ships and star charts amongst the vast array of other trinkets I've collected during my service to the Earthling Space

Corps. One of my favorites being the scale model of a cervo suit only eight inches tall that sits on my desk, my eyes scan its precision detailing. As I stare, I wonder in marvel how a modified engineering suit became the greatest division of Earth's military, not just the suit itself but also the advancements made in augmentation technology that made it one with its operator. My mind refocuses and I sit reading about the exploits of the long dead Celtic queen for about an hour, when suddenly I hear a ringing buzz come from my door.

"Who is it?" I ask awaiting a response but hear nothing. I roll my eyes and stand knowing what is on the other side of the door as I swipe the access panel. The metal door ascends to the ceiling in an instant and blocking the threshold is one of Dr. Vyers' shiny green droids hovering almost motionless until it barks at me in the voice of the doctor.

"Commander, I suggest you take this downtime to exercise. I believe Major Thorne is in the practice fields with C-squad, thank you, sir." Without even a chance to respond the audio link cuts out and the droid begins hovering back to the medical wing, a few beeps coming from it every few seconds as it disappears down the hallway.

"Doctor's orders," I say with a sigh and huff as I rub my eyes in slight frustration. *'Couldn't even give me a break, eh Doc?'*

I close the door and begin changing into my workout gear consisting of a pair of jogging pants and a long-sleeved shirt, each fitted with holes to allow access to the cervo nodes along each joint from my ankles to the base of my skull. I take several deep breaths in preparation of the pain to come as I fold my uniform and place it on the bed. Turning to the door I ping the access panel and head down the halls towards the practice yards.

Chapter 4

The Herd

I step out of the facility from the main double door entrance and instantly feel a little lighter with each step as I cross the arid grounds to the eastern practice fields. Though the moon we are on provides a small source of gravity the station requires a gravity generator located down in engineering. Although it is long overdue for an upgrade like most of Whitman Station it still functions for the most part; we find the gravity is much stronger inside the facility. I walk the bisecting paths outside through the arid patches of grass and dry dirt as I arrive at the practice yard just in time to see half the herd running in full pursuit of the other half, working their way tactically around a set of concrete barriers as both teams try for a flag tied to the top of a guard tower. My blood rushes as I see the men in their eight-foot-tall solid black glass steel suits. I see a few brace as they activate their hooves and leap high into the air reaching for the flag, each leap sending the soldier almost thirty feet into the air, a cushion of magnetic energy bursting out to soften their landing.

The Cervo-suit soldiers are the sword hand of Earth's military. Between them and I is three inches of black glass steel, a metal forged in space using man-made asteroid-like collisions to fuse harder metals. Paired with the heavy magnetic hooves is a set of hydraulic hands, delicate enough to hold an egg and powerful enough to obliterate it in an instant. Topping the black helm of these goliaths are two antler-like antennas slicked back along the top of the ears. These horns give the operator all their senses amongst other things such as infrared and night vision. So sophisticated that it can tell the user how fast and in which direction the wind is blowing, how much moisture resides in it and any other foreign particles that might be in it. Seeing them move in formation gives me chills, the slick movement of the joints, the small clang of metal as each part moves in unison, the humming sound of over a dozen fusion cores. It all brings me right back to my days on the fields, taking the fight to the serfs, where I was a real Commander.

"Commander on the field!" I hear Major Thorne yell to the troops as every soldier comes to an instant halt and salutes, pulling me from my day dreaming and back to reality.

"At ease, men, continue your drills," I say as I take a position next to Major Thorne with my arms folded in front of me, his suit towering almost two feet over me as his shadow blocks the sun from my eyes.

"Didn't think we'd see you today, sir." Thorne's voice cracks through his suit's exterior speakers.

"Well, it appears *mother* Vyers won't let up until I listen to her," I remark with a small laugh of sarcasm.

"She cares, sir, we all care," he replies with a reassuring voice as he lets his faceplate swing open showing the sincerity in his blue eyes.

"I know she cares, Adrian; my arms just aren't what they used to be," I say, stretching my aching arms out in preparation.

"That's why you need to join us more often, sir. Speaking of which, shall we go prep your C-suit?" he asks, motioning to the workshop attached to the main facility where the suits are stored and maintained.

"Yes, let's make the doctor happy," I say with a sigh and a glint of gallows humor as I head into the large steel box of a workshop. Entering in I see almost one hundred work frames, all empty of their C-suits except for a select few. As I stride to the far end of the workshop, I see a knocked-over keg that has been tapped and empty glasses sit on a storage crate next to it. "Couldn't resist, could they?" I say with a disgruntled huff as I motion to the clearly empty keg.

"Well, you know the herd, sir," he says with a jest and small nudge from his metal-clad elbow.

"Adrian, you know discipline is equal on my station and that's not about to change. Anyone who drank from that keg will be pulling an extra round of duties, understood?" I order as I look up at his pale-skinned face framed by greyish black metal.

"Loud and clear, sir. The whole herd will be pulling a double, myself included," he says, taking my order seriously and standing at attention.

"Thank you, and don't let it happen again, Major." I nod as I continue to my suit and see it for the first time in months. I'm surprised at the lack of dust on it as I peer at its systems diagnostics on a display terminal next to it.

"Clause and Hector have been maintaining it, sir." Thorne speaks up from behind me, his hooves clanging against the ground with each step. "They reworked the weight distribution so your torso and waist take more of the weight off your shoulders," he says, pointing to the screen to show off the improvements made.

"They've done well with it. Give them my personal thanks," I say, double checking the new modifications and punching in the activation codes on the access pad attached to the work frame. Within seconds a high-pitched releasing of air is audible at the mask, chest and legs of the massive machine prying open with the soft twang of metal and a small burst of pressurized air releases from the hydraulic outlets.

I feel goose flesh appear across my back and head as I approach my suit. I touch every scratch and scar across its metal frame, remembering each moment that this suit saved my life and the lives of others. *'You can do this,'* I remind myself as I turn around and step backwards, placing my feet into each hoof, my mind whirling with images of Arili, the refugees, the bunker, the blast wave of sand-glassing plasma energy. I begin to sweat profusely and breathe quickly as I rest my back into the harness, each implant's node lining up and connecting to its counterpart in the suit. Small waves of electricity rush through me as my suit aligns itself to me. Anxiety comes creeping up my spine as I tell my suit to close and finish its activation sequence. Suddenly the awkward silence is broken by my haptic glove as it lights up with an urgent link from the command center. I toggle it open as the voice of Lieutenant Donovan comes bellowing into the speakers in my suit.

"Commander Haves, you are needed in the command center stat, we have an emergency." His worried voice clicks off the comms link.

"On route to you now, Donovan," I say with a sigh of relief as I step from my suit, covered in sweat. I grab a towel off a close-by rack and begin walking out of the workshop dabbing my face dry. "At least tell the doctor I tried if she asks, but duty calls," I say with a half-smile as I turn back to Thorne briefly before heading back to the command center. He nods and smiles, understanding, as he turns off the activation procedures to my suit and rejoins the herd on the field.

Chapter 5

The Ship with No Name

I feel the gravity weigh on my shoulders as I step back into the station from the main entrance. A wall of sound hits me as I see the main atrium is now the stage for a beer pong tournament. Small groups cheering on the contenders as others take bets and enjoy their brief moment of peace in our busy year. I ascend one of the two ten-foot staircases that lead up and meet creating a landing to a single twenty-foot staircase leading to the second level. The main floor of the station is made up of mostly bunkhouses and storage rooms, the second level houses a majority of the service centers, the command center, officer's wing, medical bay and the armory. The basement level is the heart of the station as in it resides our power core, scanner reading rooms and the rail gun terminals along with the engineering command center.

I stride at a brisk pace through the vast fifteen-foot-wide hallways, the silver and black accented walls shining in the artificial light casted down from the ceiling fixtures hanging twenty feet above me. Directional maps and small communication terminals lay flat against the walls in thirty-foot intervals. Most screens are black and without power due to the upload process.

Arriving in the command center I see the skeleton crew of personnel all hunched over a terminal showing readings from the short-range scanners. I get roughly halfway across the room before Donovan notices me. He is clearly about to yell attention to the others as I motion for him to ease but it's too late.

"Officer on deck!" Donovan shouts as the other four technicians stand at attention.

"At ease, men," I order as I salute casually. "What's the situation?" I ask as I approach them, still clad in my sweat-soaked workout gear.

"Sir, something has breached the atmosphere," Donovan says as he hands me a holo-tab that shows a clear trajectory path across the northern hemisphere. "Short range scanners picked it up thirteen minutes ago and clearly shows an escalated expansion of the vapor trail but no ship is visible." I look up with a notched eyebrow of surprise. "The ship has a fuel leak, sir, and seismic readings indicate a possible crash," he says with the professional tone of a would-be officer.

"Begin a particle scan of the vapor trail, I want to know what kind of ship this is. Where did it go down?" I order bluntly, taking charge of the situation as I view the scanner charts.

"Based on the trajectory and the seismic readings, the nav charts approximate about three hours south-east of the station, sir," Donovan replies with expertise.

"Three hours on foot is about forty-five minutes for the herd," I say out loud to myself as I switch my comms link on to Major Thorne. "Thorne, we've got a possible crash site about three leaps south east of the station. Take ten men and get eyes on the site. Prepare for a possible search and rescue." My comms buzz for a moment.

"Copy that, sir, we are Oscar Mike in five." His comm link blinks off as I turn my attention back to Donovan.

"Inform Dr. Vyers of the situation and have her prep the med bay for any potential patients," I say with a cold voice. "Or potential bodies."

Donovan gives me a nod and begins his duties as I go to my terminal and start a case file for the situation. Several minutes pass as I fill out the paperwork for a downed ship, losing myself to my thoughts I glance over at the countdown for the upload as it reads twenty-one hours and thirty-some minutes. I blink back to reality as the sharp voice of Corporal Skyes fills the air.

"Sir, the particle scan of the vapor trail is complete. It's clear there is a leak in the fuel line but more interesting is the trace amounts of polonium in the fuel," she says in a voice peaked with interest.

"Polonium? Only command vessels have that kind of fuel mixture," I say with a perplexed tone and pull my haptic glove up to my mouth and channel Thorne on the comms. "Major, what's your status? That ship has polonium in its fuel cells, could be from high command." Moments of dead air pass by before the comms come alive.

"Commander, we've got a mess here. The crash site spans over four klicks and the ship is practically dust. We have one survivor in critical and he is being prepped for evac now." The tone in his voice tells me things are not good.

My terminal blinks with a link to Thorne's body cam; it's blurry but soon focuses. I see wreckage spanning beyond the view of the camera lens. Small fires blaze around black charred gouges dug into the ground. His body cam turns downwards and I see a grizzled greying bearded man in a pilot's suit being prepped on a stretcher. He's unconscious and bleeding through a bandage around the top of his head.

"No one else, Major?" I ask hoping for some good news.

"None intact, sir." His answer is simple and to the point.

"Understood, Major. Do a final sweep of the area and return to base. We will have a clean-up crew on route in an hour," I say, saddened with the loss of life, and click my comms off and send the camera footage to Donovan's terminal.

"See if you can analyze the wreckage and recreate the ship," I order as I add this new information to my report and begin a routine search through our files for any missions in this sector we may have been unaware of but find nothing.

Over an hour passes before the herd arrives back with the gurney hovering amongst them. I can see them approach from the exterior cameras overlooking the main entrance in the command center. I toggle my comms to Dr. Vyers to brief her. "Claire, your patient has arrived I will be down in a few minutes to observe."

"Thank you, Commander. My droids are ready and waiting," she chimes back in her robotic voice.

I leave command to Donovan and make my way to the medical wing. I catch up with Major Thorne and two Lieutenant cervo units, Spurs and Drake, as they walk briskly with the gurney. Laying across I can see an unconscious man in a battered green flight suit with a respirator strapped across his mouth and another bandage that he has bled through on his head. I look to his vital readings and see they are nearly flat.

"He should be dead; he's a tough one, sir," Lieutenant Spurs says as he injects the man in the neck with a small dose of adrenaline to keep his heart beating.

"Tough, or lucky?" I say rhetorically as we enter into the medical wing and see the operation table prepped and Dr. Vyers fully garbed in scrubs as her droids float around her, small claws protruding from open slits in their bellies holding medical equipment.

"My droids will take it from here, thank you, Major and Commander," she says as she shoos us away with several flicks of her hands and turns to her duties.

Chapter 6

Fawkes

I'm alone in the observation room as Dr. Vyers works on the patient. He's barely alive but I've seen this woman work miracles before. Lieutenant Howell, a cervo unit, once took a magnetic blast to his pelvis while unsuited when a fellow soldier's hoof malfunctioned. Dr. Vyers managed to recreate his entire bone structure from the waist down and surgically implanted him with an artificial set. The man should have never walked again, yet I saw him running drills only a couple of hours ago. If she could do that, then I'm positive she can save this man.

"Commander, my initial scans are complete. Some very interesting things here, sir. This man has trace amounts of lead in his blood and skin, an indication of amateur tattoo work," she says with a shrill voice.

"What makes you think it's tattoos?" I ask with a confused tone.

"It's rather burned but there is one on his neck that is getting high readings," she returns in her monotone voice. "Here, see for yourself," she says curiously as she orders one of her droids to get a closer look, its camera view streaming on my holo-tab.

I look at the scorched mark on the man's neck inquisitively as my eyes squint trying to fill in the blanks; I can make out what looks like the wing of a predator bird and the top half of a sickle.

"He could be a mercenary, Claire. That could be the crest of the *Raven Fire* mercenary company," I state bluntly as my teeth grind hard as I'm not quite fond of men who fight for money.

"He also has a military insignia over his heart, sir, and x-rays show he is implanted with cervo nodes, but his skin has begun to grow over the implants. He must have spent years without a suit." *'Couldn't have mentioned that first!'* I think to myself as I roll my eyes at what she considers important information.

"What is the insignia?" I ask concerned and frustrated.

"I believe it's for the twelfth hundred airborne herd, sir," she says as she continues her work.

I go quiet as I swipe the holo-tab in my hands and search the records for the twelfth hundred airborne herd division. I look for dishonorable discharges and find three case files. Two are clearly not the man on the table but the last one looks a lot like him without the beard. A vast majority of his service records has been blacked out and classified, but what I can gather I find very interesting. *'Gregory Fawkes, age forty-nine, Commander of the twelfth hundred Airborne division. Thirty-seven successful drop missions and overall loss of fifteen soldiers. Present at Haverford, Bilemy and Parinvox. Discharged and imprisoned for negligence and disobeying direct orders from High Command. Sentenced to three years on Lunar prison Seti-5. Released eleven years ago. Known affiliations: Raven Fire Mercenaries. Current whereabouts unknown.'* My jaw drops and my face grows pale as I press the speaker button to the operation room. "Claire, I need you to handcuff him to the bed," I say in a flat authoritative tone without hesitation.

"What's the matter, sir?" she asks, looking up over her mask and glasses with worry in her eyes.

"He's a decommissioned cervo, did hard time during the war but a lot of his file is blacked out, could be for war crimes. Just do as I ask please," I order through the speaker with ever-growing curiosity as to who this man is.

She stops her work, placing her instruments next to her on a plate held by one of her droids and walks to a cabinet across the room. From it I see her draw two sets of heavy steel handcuffs. She crosses back to the man on the bed and chains him to it from the wrists. I pull the holo-tab back up and begin looking for more information on this man. Several minutes pass when my comms buzz and I see another urgent link from Donovan.

"Update," I order simply as I open the comm link.

"Commander, we made a recreation of the ship based off our readings and the scans from the crash site," Donovan says through the speaker. "It appears to be a ship registered to the Earthling Intelligence Command."

"EIC? You're positive, Donovan?" I ask, perplexed, as my heart pumps faster and my mind tries to make connections. Earthling Intelligence Command is the covert counterspy branch of the military, their ships are coated with certain epoxies so as to not be picked up on scanners. The only reason our short-range scanners tagged them was because of their fuel leak.

"We are ninety percent positive, sir. The hull was coated with titanium alloy and epoxy residue and the clear presence of polonium in the fuel cells shows that it has to be EIC, sir," Donovan reports back with assuredness in his voice. *'He's usually not wrong,'* I remind myself as he finishes.

"Thank you, Lieutenant. Add it to the report and continue a search through our database for any possible missions in this sector. I may have missed when I looked," I say, cutting the link, wishing I could call Laramie Station and have all of this sorted in a matter of minutes.

Over an hour passes before Dr. Vyers stabilizes Fawkes and

leaves the operating room. I peer at the man on the bed. His vitals appear back to normal and a fresh bandage has been wrapped across his head. She enters the observation room in dirty scrubs spackled in blood, one of her droids hovering behind her like a silent companion as she stands near the disposal box.

"What's his condition?" I ask as she pulls her gloves off and removes her mask.

"The patient has seen blunt-force trauma to most of his body and has several contusions and lacerations on his neck and head. He is concussed and needed seventeen stiches but he is resting for now. His flight suit saved his life, sir," she says empathetically as she disposes of her dirty gown in a bin against the wall and walks to her terminal to input her surgical data and add it to the report.

"Cervos are hard to kill, even without a suit," I say, cringing at the notion that this man was once like me. "When can I question him?" I ask next with my arms folded, antsy to get this issue dealt with and back to my down time.

"When he awakens, sir," she says, trying to guard her patient's wellbeing as she glances over her shoulder from her terminal.

"He's a prisoner, Claire, not a patient," I say, demanding a better answer.

"I can give him a small injection of stimulant in a half an hour, sir," she says with a huff as she stands and pulls her holo-tab from my hands and brings it to her face so she doesn't have to look me in the eyes. "I'll inform you when I make the injection," she says as she turns and syncs her data to her tablet.

"I'll wait," I say bluntly as I stand in front of the window of the observation room and watch this criminal's vital readings, counting the minutes and seconds as they pass.

As I wait alone in the observation room for the injection I watch as the doctor's droids maintain the IV drips and pain relievers being administered to Mr. Fawkes. *'What the hell is EIC doing out here? Why wouldn't they inform us? Maybe they tried but with outward communications down it didn't come through. None of this makes any sense.'* I ponder relentlessly to myself then open a link with both Majors and debrief them on the situation.

"Why would EIC not inform us of a ship in the sector?" Pirez asks over the sound of arc welders and shouting engineers.

"They technically don't have to under section three of the unified information act. Also, who is this Fawkes guy?" Thorne chimes in with curiosity.

"He's a cervo turned prisoner then turned mercenary so my guess is as good as yours. The ship could be stolen but it's all speculation till Vyers gives the stimulant shot and I can question him properly. Nonetheless, something brought that ship down. Sasha, I know we have no long-range scanners, but is there anything we can do to get a reading?" I talk over the both of them and take charge over their constant questions.

"We could potentially amplify the sonar scanners. Honestly, it's a long shot but it could give us some picture," she suggests in a guessing tone after thinking to herself for several moments.

"See what you can do and put your best guys on it," I order as I click off her link. "Thorne, call the cleaning crew back from the crash site. I don't want to take any chances if they're out there and something happens, understood?" I finish.

"Loud and clear, sir. Calling the herd home now," he says before ending his comm link.

I spend several more minutes pulling up file logs on a holo-tab, looking for anything that may indicate this ship's mission or a potential theft ticket for the ship. My eyes are glued to the luminescent screen. I pour through backlog after backlog looking for any indication of this mission or any mentions of this Mr. Fawkes. I find his incarceration files: they don't tell me much more than I already know but he has been diagnosed with rage issues and was placed in solitary confinement away from other prisoners. I begin to sweat as I read more and more but find nothing of actual use when I hear Dr. Vyers enter the operating room. I look up and see her preparing a syringe next to the unconscious prisoner. I set down the holo-tab and leave the observation room and enter the bright operation room as she injects the man with the stimulant. I wait as she watches his vital reading from the display, her droids hovering around performing scans of his chest and head. My heart begins beating faster in my chest with anticipation as I watch his blood pressure and other vitals begin to rise. Suddenly the man convulses for a few moments. His eyes don't open but he throws himself around in pure hysteria. Within seconds he eases down and his eyes open, piercing blue eyes peering around as he looks at the doctor and me in pure confusion.

"Where am I?" he asks with a coarse dry voice.

"What's your name?" I retort without even acknowledging his question.

"Fawkes, Gregory Fawkes," he says slowly as he tries to pull his hand to the bandage on his head but finds his hands chained and looks up at me in confusion.

"Thank you for your honesty, Mr. Fawkes. Off to a good start. I am Commander Haves of Whitman Station. Now tell me why a discharged cervo was piloting an intelligence class cruiser," I say without remorse. His eyes quake and his brow furrows at my reference to his discharge.

"I need to get a message to Laramie Station," he says with a thousand-yard stare into my eyes.

"Not gonna happen. Tell me why you were out here," I bark with intimidation as his eyes drop down and he grows quiet for several deep breaths.

"My crew was hired through EIC; they gave us the ship," he says without looking up.

"Crew? You mean the Raven Fire mercenaries then, I assume?" I scoff at the thought of being a gun for hire.

"What other work could a guy like me get?" he asks rhetorically.

"What was your mission?" I ask, trying to find any holes in his story, my arms folded as I loom over the foot of his bed.

"We were told to investigate anomalies in the asteroid belt that your station's long-range scanners were picking up," he says without hesitation.

"Bullshit, we aren't look for anomalies in the asteroid belt," I say with a grin as I find his lie.

"Maybe you weren't, but they were," he says as he raises his eyes to mine and stares.

"Why the hell would EIC hire mercs and not tell us of this mission?" I blast out, losing my cool slightly.

"I believe section three of the unifi—" he begins to say as I cut him off.

"I know about section three. What did you find there?" I ask, regaining my composure.

"Thousands," is all he says with a dead stare burning holes in my eyes.

"Thousands of what?" I say slowly as my heart beats uncontrollably.

"Ships, Commander," he says with a frightful voice.

"Thousands of ships in the asteroid belt?" I say with a laugh. "You know, you really had me going for a second there, Fawkes. You know what I think happened? I think you stole this ship with your crew but botched the job when the fuel line ruptured. Or maybe you came across some pirates that blew you out of the sky. Sound accurate? Sounds far more accurate than thousands of ships sitting in the chaos of the asteroid belt. Hmm? Right?" I say as I loom over him with an over-bearing presence. I don't want to believe him but his expressions look extremely sincere.

"I'm telling you the truth, Commander," he replies with a flat impatient tone.

"EIC will be the judge of that," I say as I look to Dr. Vyers who has been waiting patiently beside the bed. "Doctor, please make Mr. Fawkes here comfortable. Once the upload is complete we will have a prisoner transport called in." I turn and begin to leave the room as Fawkes yells and struggles in his bed, the handcuffs rattling and banging against the bed.

"It won't matter! We'll all be dead by then! They were following us! They were following us!" His voice grows more and more distant as I make my way down the halls of the medical wing.

Chapter 7

It's Just a Cloud

I walk the halls of the main bunk area and can hear nothing but fun being had. Looking into each bunk as I pass to see small groups of soldiers and engineers enjoying their downtime. Although the yearly upload is a hassle it has become somewhat of a holiday on the station; ninety percent of the station is off duty for the day so they throw small parties and let loose a little. I pass one room with three engineers doing rounds of shots. They offer one to me but I simply nod my head an cheer them on with a thumbs up and continue my walk of the facility heading for the command center. I turn the corner onto the stretch of hall leading to the massive steel double doors of the command center when my haptic glove begins to ping with a comms link from Pirez. I accept the request and acknowledge her.

"Commander, you need to come down here now. We managed to amplify the sonar scanner and picked up something strange that you may want to see," she mumbles on and begins talking to an engineer in the background when the link ends abruptly. *'Not what I want to hear.'*

I double time it across the station trying not to alert anyone I pass as I head down to the lower levels where the heart of the station resides. I descend into the belly of Whitman Station and pass rows of terminals for the orbital rail gun belt. The engineers for systems like this are not very different from cervo soldiers;

they are implanted through their hands and brain to integrate with the terminals and to control upwards of fifteen guns at a time and with a high accuracy rating. Just past the long rows of terminals is the entrance to the ion cannons loading bay. It was designed to be able to be operated by a single person, although since the Scudinski incident we prefer a two-man team. Turning right I see an open door to one of the scanner's reading rooms and see Pirez and three technicians huddled over a terminal. She looks up and sees me approaching as she steps away and meets me half way.

"Commander, we were able to amplify the sonar scanner like you asked. It create an image every fifteen minutes but it's something," she says, adjusting her hair tie, something she only does when she is nervous.

"Explain in full detail, Major," I say as I approach and peer over the bright green screen with what looks like puffy clouds of white being illuminated amongst a sea of green.

"This reading says something very big is out there, sir. We've gotten three readings so far and it looks like it's moving, sir," she says as she shows the images one after the other, showing a clear movement pattern.

"What could it be?" I ask calmly as my mind runs a mile a minute with fear and anxiety.

"We can't tell much aside from the fact that it's there. It really could just be a nebulous cloud thick with heavy metal particles for all we know, but the sonar wasn't meant to scan outside the atmosphere," she says in a serious tone.

"Can we get a trajectory?" I ask, hoping for a good answer.

"Honestly, sir, it lines up almost with that of the ship that crashed earlier today." Her words make my heart sink as I feel a cold shiver crawl up my spine.

"This information is now top level and doesn't leave this

room, understood?" I say to everyone present. "I want an update every fifteen minutes, and please get me some distancing statistics; I want to know how long we have," I say to Pirez as I make for the door and out of engineering back to the medical wing. *'So glad I have that girl on my team.'*

Major Pirez was top of all her classes in the academy; her genius was visible from infancy. Where most children spend the ages of twelve to twenty learning subjects such as medicine, art, science, and many other vocations before choosing a career at the age of twenty-one, Sasha at the age of thirteen had already received a degree in technical engineering. She joined the service at eighteen and was already a Lieutenant when she arrived on Whitman, her expertise gaining her the rank of Major within a year. *'She saved us from the gas leak, and now she's proven herself again.'*

My mind is racing as I speed walk through the halls back to the medical wing. The idea that a mass of ships could be hidden in the asteroid belt is preposterous. Although very little of it has been mapped, it's pure chaos out there. Even during the time of the *Great Expansion*, there were few ships to ever attempt to chart the asteroid fields; great heroes were lost in insane attempts to be the first to map the unstable frontier. *'Maybe it's a serf fleet that doesn't know the war is over,'* I think to myself as I arrive in the medical office, storming past the humming droids and a startled Dr. Vyers and into the operating room where I see Fawkes sitting quietly. Our eyes meet as I cross the room and begin to unlock his chains.

"Tell me everything you know," I demand as I pull out a pair of coveralls from a locker in the corner and toss them on the foot of the bed.

"You believe me now?" he asks in quiet disbelief as he gets

up rubbing his wrists and starts to change.

"I make my choices based on information available and the information we've obtained bares similarities to your account. I'm willing to hear you out properly, now tell me everything you know," I order in a professional yet apologetic tone as I turn to let him dress himself. *I'm not going to say sorry; I'm just doing my job.'*

"We had just arrived at the Vindow Crest of the asteroid belt here in Epsilon Eridani. The ship was set with dozens of outward scanners to reduce the need for optic view ports. Our scanners were getting strange readings, like hundreds of vapor trails or a giant gas ball of exhaust. We opened the view ports to try and get some sense of things and there it was, a mass of ships twice the size of the invasion force of Bilemy," he says in the practiced tone of the officer he once was.

"What class of ships were they? Is it the serfs?" I question as I turn to see him fully dressed in his grey coveralls.

"For all we know it was serfs, but they didn't respond to any communication requests. They swarmed us in seconds from just about every direction, almost like they were expecting us. They were mostly defunct fighter class ships. We shot down some thirty or so before we were overwhelmed and had to flee." He stands there almost as if he's awaiting a command. "Can I please send a message to Laramie Station? They might be able to clear a lot of this up," he pleads as I stand there still not sure how to comprehend this new information.

"I wasn't lying when I said that's not going to happen; we have our yearly upload today and communications are down for another seventeen hours," I say as his face grows pale.

"Then we are all as good as dead," he says with a flat emotionless tone as he sits on the edge of the bed with his face in his hands.

I leave him to wallow in his fear for a moment as I pull up my haptic glove and order both Pirez and Thorne to the medical wing for a briefing. It takes several minutes as Fawkes and I stand in awkward silence. I can feel his eyes on me, not sure if he is judging or admiring. Pirez arrives first in her dirty green jumper, her olive-skin face smeared with grease and dry sweat. Thorne arrives moments later in his C-suit with his facemask open, his stern pale face turning to Fawkes as he enters.

"Is he no longer a prisoner, sir?" Thorne asks through narrowed eyes as he does an ocular pat-down of Fawkes.

"Mr. Fawkes here has given me information that matches the readings Major Pirez has obtained through the sonar scans." My eyes dart between the both of them as they stand there taking in what I have to say. "If it's true, then we have an armada arriving soon," I say with a frightful tone.

"Sir, we still don't know what our readings are. It could still be a heavy metal cloud for all we know," she argues frantically, not wanting to accept this new knowledge.

"A cloud shot down a ship, Sasha? Is that truly more believable? Come now, I thought you had more sense than that," I say in a harsh fatherly tone as Thorne speaks up.

"Then what's the plan, sir?" he asks in a ready and waiting voice.

"Call the herd, I'll make the announcement," I say in my officer's bravado.

Chapter 8

Vacations Over

The PA system crackles to life and blares over the entire facility. *"This is Commander Haves. I need everyone to stop what they are doing and gather in the atrium for a briefing immediately. Holiday is cancelled."* I march down the halls to the atrium with Majors Pirez and Thorne as Fawkes trails behind with our escort of cervo soldiers, their hooves pounding in unison as we arrive. Entering from the second floor I descend the twenty-foot staircase to the landing where it splits into the left and right staircases overlooking the main entrance. I see the entire crew of the station standing around wondering what's going on; some are half asleep and others are half in the bag but all stand at attention when we arrive. It's quiet enough to hear a pin drop as I begin to speak to my entire crew of two hundred and forty-three.

"Forty-nine minutes after we began our upload this morning, an intelligence class cruiser went down three hours south of the facility. On board was a crew of mercenaries hired by EIC, captained by this man." I point to Fawkes as his eyes dart to avoid the glares of every staff member. "Mr. Fawkes' mission was to investigate anomalies in the asteroid field that our station was unaware of, and it appears the anomaly was an armada of some thousand fighter class ships in varying states of disrepair. We are unsure at this point if this is a second serf uprising or something else, but I can tell you that this fleet is heading our way." I tap my haptic glove and a large holographic image of our sonar scan appears floating above the crew and brightens the entire atrium, the large green square casting an eerie glow on everyone's faces. "From what readings we can get thanks to the great work of Major Pirez and her team, it appears they are aligned with a direct course to our station. In two hours, they will be within range of our short-range scanners; this will give us a better image of what we are dealing with. Once they are in range of our local communications, we will attempt to hail them on all frequencies and if they do not respond we must therefore assume them to be hostile. After hostilities are confirmed, the rail gun technicians will open fire with orbital volleys from the gun belt, and if the volleys fail to subdue this fleet, we may have a ground invasion on our hands." I look around at the faces of these young soldiers and engineers. "I know for a majority of you, your only combat experience is from basic training and the rare pirate attack. That may change today. As I am opening the armories and issuing the defensive measures protocol, I expect all of you to fight, no exceptions." I can see their fear as they shift on their heels, some trying to hide tears. "If we don't hold them here, this armada could ruin half the Oregon Trail before anyone knows what's going on. We have prepared an automated message to be sent out once the upload is complete in sixteen hours; our objective is to ensure the communications array stays intact. We have about five hours to prepare. All cervo units will be under the command of Major Thorne, all railgun operators and essential engineers will be with Major Pirez, the remainder will be with me. First order is for everyone to go to the armory and be fitted with your battle gear and rail rifles. The cervos will help you. Now, go to it." I end my speech and turn to Major Thorne as I point to Fawkes. "Get that man in a C-suit," I say as I make my way to the medical wing.

"I haven't been in a suit in years," he says with a hint of self-doubt.

"Me either," I say bluntly as I turn to two cervo soldiers. "Clause, Drake, you two come with me," I order as I walk them with me to the medical wing, their heavy boots clanging with each step.

I don't need them for what I'm about to do, I'm only bringing them to keep Dr. Vyers in line as she seems to think she outranks me on certain decisions. We arrive in the eggshell white halls of the medical wing in minutes, its long picture windows now blocked by the thick steel solar blinds activated by the defensive measures protocol. I arrive at the door with my cervos in tow behind me and see Dr. Vyers prepping her triage room for potential wounded soldiers. She looks up, startled, at the sudden appearance of the cervo soldiers.

"What's going on, Commander? What is the meaning of this?" she asks as she steps back as the soldiers walk over to her droids and begin punching in commands on their holo-tabs.

"Sorry, Doctor, but with the protocol I have to commandeer your droids for field duty," I say with my hands behind my back and a stern unbreakable face.

"This is preposterous, Commander, they are medical droids not your soldiers! They would serve a far better purpose here than amongst gunfire!" she begins shouting as I cut her off.

"They are field medic droids built for open operation and active duty; their scanners can detect a heartbeat at a half a klick. We need as many eyes as we can get, Claire, and these are military property not your pets, is that clear?" I bark at her.

"This is an abuse of command, I would very mu—" she begins but I cut her off.

"This is an order, Doctor, if you choose not to follow it you will be imprisoned and await trial for breach of command and potential treason. I am only doing what we need to survive, Claire, do we have an understanding?" I glare into her eyes and lean forward a little.

"Yes, sir, understood, sir," she says with clear sarcasm but doesn't fight the inevitable.

"Thank you, Doctor," I say as I turn my attention to my soldiers. "I want one on the roof over-looking the main entrance, one near the scrap heap near the back end of engineering at the gun belt and the last one on the east side over-looking the practice yards. Is that understood, soldiers?" I ask, knowing their response as they both salute and get to work. I look back at the doctor as I turn to leave the room, her eyes not leaving her holo-tab as I'm sure she's writing up a complaint to High Command. I laugh to myself knowing it won't mean much in a few hours. Command hasn't listened to any of my complaints, so why on earth would they listen to hers?

Chapter 9

Lock, Stock and Ten Thousand Rounds

I walk the halls of the bunk area no longer hearing cheers and revelry, instead hearing boots on the ground and orders being given. We've run drills of the defensive protocol before but it has a far more eerie feeling when it's the real thing. These are children I see running around in loose fitting battle plates, being shown and re-shown how to arm their rail rifles. Some practice hand signals, some pray and others smoke cigarettes in silence. I can see the fear building in their eyes as they prepare barricades and plan defensive routes around the station. An array of small mazes and choke points have been set up as I make my inspection; multi-level platforms of scaffolding and blast-resistant metal sheets make the once wide halls feel so small and narrow.

My inspection brings me back around to the main atrium where I see a long line of concrete barriers and sandbags being piled three feet high and backed by metal blast shields. Soldiers are practicing maneuvers with cervo units at their station, most in awe at the suits as they rarely get to see them up close. I see Major Thorne looking over schematics of the facility near the main door to the station. He turns and acknowledges me with a salute as I approach.

"Commander, I'd like to discuss our defensive capabilities." He shows me his holo-tab with an outline of the station. The station is designed like two square-shaped figure eights with a long hall on the western side leading to the hangar.

"Of course, Major," I say as I take the offered holo-tab from his hands. "Lock down and cut power to the tertiary housing area leaving only emergency power to the local turret systems. Put the entire first floor on lockdown, seal all emergency doors and cut power to all but emergency systems. If they get in, they can only go up not under, understood? I want the main atrium to be our first line of defense with retreat points located at the command center and the entry way to engineering. If each point fails then we make an expeditious retreat for the hangar. Please ensure all cervos are aware of this order and pass it on the regular soldiers, understood?" I order to him as I mark the points on the holo-tab.

"Of course, but what about the hangar, sir?" he asks with concern on his voice.

"Lock it down and cut power to everything but our entryway. The blast door can withstand a dozen ion blasts from orbit; it will be our final stand if we need it," I order back without looking up. Our hangar was built to house over two hundred fighter class ships. It was fully armed during the war but today only houses five low-atmospheric recon class ships which are neither capable of leaving the atmosphere nor armed well enough to put up a worthy fight and one officer's transport vessel built for space travel but it can only fit a half dozen personnel.

"Yes, sir, thank you, sir," he says as he salutes and begins passing my orders to the herd. "There is one other thing, sir, if I may?" he says sheepishly in a tone I rarely hear from him.

"Of course, Major." I nod in approval.

"Several technicians from the hangar were asking about the officer's transport, asking if anyone will be let go to get a message out?" He stammers a bit as he talks, clearly nervous to ask such a question.

"They want to flee? We need every able body possible," I state in a quiet anger so as to not attract attention. *'Cowards like that wouldn't have lasted one tour on Arili,'* I think to myself as Thorne continues.

"I don't approve of the idea of fleeing, sir, but sending the ship with a message could be our saving grace. Even if we all die here, at least there is a chance someone will find out what happened," he states clearly with anticipation of my response on his face, a response I dwell on for several moments.

"Between you and Major Pirez, I'd like you to select two pilots and a navigator for this mission. Upload all the data we have collected so far on the situation into the ship and tell them to make for The Rock at full speed. Select no cervos or crucial personnel, is that understood?" I say with reluctance, knowing that three men alone could make or break an entire battle.

"Clearly, sir, and thank you," Thorne says as he makes a grand salute.

I nod sternly and continue my inspection down to engineering; I pass several heaps of sandbags and steel barriers being set into position. I pass dozens of my soldiers and engineers. Some nod to me as I pass, others won't even look me in the eyes as I descend the stairs into engineering. The empty terminals I passed only hours ago are now online and humming with bright displays as I see the rail gun operators sit and integrate with their machines, their fingers and eyes moving miles as they breathe slowly and sit in their seats. I pass by them and see Lieutenant Mackie and Corporal Welsh step into the ion cannon's firing booth, continuing down the hall and entering the heart of engineering. A smaller version of the command center built for the singular purpose of keeping this station alive, it's there at the main terminal that I see Major Pirez standing in her black and grey battle suit with a clean rail rifle slung across her back. Her eyes peer up from her command console and see me approaching from her left. A few wisps of her dark brown hair dangle over her face, having come loose from her ponytail.

"Commander, I need to speak with you in private if that's all right?" she asks as she motions to her small messy office. I nod and usher her first as we enter and close the door. Stacks of technical books and unfinished projects are strewn about her cubicle.

"What's going on?" I ask with concern as she leans against the edge of her desk with a look of concern on her face.

"Sir, we are fully stocked with ten thousand rounds of ammunition for the rail gun belt. Our ammunition allocation is based off the ability to fight the biggest fleet ever amassed, which of course you know was the invasion force of Bilemy," she says as her voice ramps up to a flustered speech. Bilemy was a serf-controlled planet that required a fleet of over two-thousand ships to be successfully invaded and reclaimed in the name of Earth.

"I'm aware, Sasha, so what's the issue?" I ask with concern as I rarely see her react in this manner. It doesn't bode well when my officers act like this; fear is a powerful thing.

"I've run the number ten times, sir." She pauses and takes a deep breath. "Based on the size of this fleet, we have seven minutes of ammunition." Her face pales and her eyes avert mine as she stands there, quaking in fear of my potential reaction.

"That's...that's impossible, Sasha, only seven minutes? There must be a miscalculation," I say, perplexed and almost outraged at this news, but I remain calm to keep her from losing it.

"No miscalculations, I assure you, sir. If we made nothing

but critical hits on the vessels, we may be able to stretch it to nine minutes. I have the ammo presses on and working overtime, even then we may only get another thousand rounds!" she says, running the numbers again on her holo-tab.

"Calm yourself, Sasha. How long do we have until they are in range of the short-ranged scanners?" I ask, trying to divert her thoughts; the last thing I need is my lead engineer off her game.

"Maybe an hour, Commander," she says bluntly.

"When we get a better picture of what's coming I want a full briefing immediately. Perhaps we can focus fire when they get closer for a better chance at prime hits?" I ponder to her as she collects herself.

"That may work, but based on the size of this fleet I guarantee we won't get them all," she says reluctantly with a disheartened voice.

"That's what the herd is for," I say, placing a hand on her shoulder. "We are going to get through this, Sasha." I've seen a squad of ten cervos tear through a serf stronghold of over two hundred and come out unscathed; I can trust in what they are capable of.

"Thank you, Commander," she says as her comms go off, calling her back to the engineering center. She salutes as we leave her office.

I watch over the engineers at their terminals as my comms go off with an urgent link from Major Thorne. I key the link open and am startled by the sounds of shouting in the background.

"Sir, we've got a situation brewing in the hangar. You need to get down here now!" Thorne shouts.

"I'm on my way, Adrian," I reply quickly and bolt for the hangar.

Chapter 10

Drawing Lots

I arrive in the hangar to see a few dozen personnel surrounding the transport vessel. Two cervo units stand in front of the access door as the soldiers try to push past them. They are shouting profanities as I spot Thorne trying to calm the crowd. I push through the group to get to him.

"What the hell is going on?" I shout over the yells and pleading of the crowd.

"I'm sorry, sir, but they all caught wind of the plan to send the ship and they all want passage," he says through his suit's speakers as I climb onto a storage container overlooking them all.

"Enough!" I yell over them as they all stop and stare with dread in their eyes. "Who orchestrated this?" I ask in anger as they all look shamefully away except for one that puts his hand in the air.

"I did!" shouts Corporal Barnes, a hangar technician. "I think it's bullshit that you're only sending three people when we could easily stuff a dozen people in there," he yells at me with anger as I shake my head in disappointment.

"I didn't realize I was surrounded by so many cowards," I say, looking around at every soldier present. Most don't even want to look at me as I press the issue.

"Some of us have families, we shouldn't have to die for nothing!" Barnes shouts back immediately.

"I'm not asking you to die for nothing, I'm asking you all to fulfill the oaths you made as soldiers of Earth." I try to reason with them.

"Fuck the oath," Barnes yells but immediately regrets his choice of words when he sees my reaction.

"Fuck the oath? That's treason, Corporal, I could have you court martialed just for saying that," I remind him as I continue. "Does anyone know what Cortez did when he landed in South America? Hmm? Anyone? He burned his ships to show his men that there was no going back! I am not Cortez, but I could have the herd tear that ship apart if I hear one more second of treasonous talk." I take a deep breath and look to every single person in front of me. "Now, who wants to flee?" I ask as I see almost thirty hands bolt into the air. "All right, now who thinks they deserve to be on that ship?" I pose to them as not a single hand wavers in the air. "Fine, I'm sure you all have your reasons but it's not going to happen. Three people are getting on that ship, not a single soul more," I say as the crowd grows rowdy again, but Thorne steps forward and puts his speakers on full blast.

"Silence when the Commander is talking!" he bellows so loud the words echo and bounce across the massive hangar as everyone quiets. Only the shuffle of frightened feet can be heard.

"Thank you, Major," I say after things go quiet and continue. "As I was saying, three people will be getting on that ship and if think that our officer's choice is biased or plays favorites then we will do this the old fashion way. Major Thorne, go get the stones." I motion to Thorne who goes to a storage area and comes back with a heavy bag and begins walking amongst the crowd. "In this bag are many black stones and three white stones. Pull a rock and hold it in your closed hand until I say otherwise." I watch with crossed arms as Thorne works his way through them, each taking a stone in their fists until everyone has one. "All right, now open your hands," I say as they all look to their open palms.

Cries ring out from some of the female soldiers as they look at the black stones in their hands, profanities shouted from others. I see Lieutenant Marcovich with a white stone in his hand as on his shoulder his wife cries with a black stone in hers. I see him look at the stone in his hand then at his sobbing wife as he looks up to me.

"Commander? Permission to give my stone to Corporal Marcovich?" he says with the face of a man accepting his fate and knowing what must be done to protect what he loves.

"You see that, everyone? Now that is a soldier of Earth! A man giving up his chance at survival so that he can protect what he loves most. Permission granted. Corporal Marcovich, you'll be on that ship," I say as she hugs her husband passionately and they exchange admiration of their love for each other.

"Thank you, sir," she says through tears as her and the two other white stone holders are escorted to the ship.

"Open the hangar," I order as the massive ceiling above us whirls to life and pries open like the maw of some giant beast. We all watch as the ship activates its thrusters and takes off into the sky and disappears into the atmosphere. I look back at the remaining soldiers with their paled faces. "Now that that's dealt with, I don't want to hear one more second of this, is that understood?" I take a deep breath and pause for a moment. "I know the fear that comes with the realities of war. You all must understand that we need every single hand we can use. Now I want you all to get back to your stations and prepare for battle or I will put you on the front lines in the atrium! Dismissed!" I shout as they all begin to trickle back to their stations, some accepting their fates and others still shaking their heads in disappointment and disbelief.

Chapter 11

Bilemy

I leave the hangar through the way I came in, passing the rail gun terminals, and see the technicians prepping their targeting directives as pings of acknowledgment beep from each terminal one by one. I pull up my holo-tab from my pocket and begin a search for historical battles where soldiers were outnumbered; thousands of search results come streaming in from our database. One entry catches my attention immediately as I was just reading about it hours ago: *The Battle of Watling Street* where the forces of Boudicca fell to the Romans. Eighty thousand fell to the Roman forces of only ten thousand due to a funnel-like tactic that Romans used to stop the enemy from circling them. *'Meeting them in the open will get us torn apart by their sheer numbers. The station will funnel them… Hopefully.'*

I continue to fortify a strategy using the insight of battles past as I work my way through the maze of barricades until I reach the far side of the facility, where I arrive at the entrance to the C-suit workshop. I see the place is barren and deserted as the herd has taken what they need for their defensive positions. I walk past the stalls and their empty work frames as I grow closer to my suit. In the stall next to mine is a cervo unit sitting with his head down.

"Shouldn't you be prepping, soldier?" I ask with my commander's bravado as the head looks up at me, its facemask open as I see Fawkes staring at me with his thousand-yard stare. "How long has it been?" I ask, knowing he's been years without a suit.

"Fourteen years," he says with a dead voice as his eyes waver with embarrassment.

"Three for me," I respond bluntly and motion to my machine. "Come give me a hand," I order as I walk over to my cervo suit and begin the activation procedures on the keypad next to the frame. "Why did they take it?" I ask over my shoulder as he stands and approaches behind me, the soft thuds of his hooves echoing in the empty warehouse.

"I'm sure my file says it all," he says in a deep voice clearly not wanting to talk about it, but I'm going to make him talk about it.

"Not much actually, most was blacked out and classified. I want to hear your side of it," I say as the fusion core of my suit whirls to life with a low hum. He goes quiet and shuffles in place, then begins to speak after a moment.

"We were a twenty-suit recon unit on Bilemy, dropped in via low-altitude gliders into the outskirts of the Crissium Valley to investigate a potential serf stronghold." He looks at me awaiting a question but everyone knows about the Crissium stronghold; it's the reason the Bilemy fleet was created. I nod and let him continue as my suit's chest, legs and mask open with a soft release of pressure and steam. "We were fifteen klicks in along a ridge overlooking the forested encampment, goddamn thing looked like Camelot from those ancient stories. High concrete towers, thick steel reinforced walls, and an anti-air array that would put this place to shame." He blows air from his nostrils with a huff of reluctance but continues as I step backwards into my machine with my eyes locked on his. "Auto turrets opened fire as we began scans of the area and pinned us along the ridge. We attempted a retreat but ended up being separated with thirteen men still trapped. We called air support and they arrived to pick us up at the evac site, but they denied the request to send a transport for my trapped men," he says flat as my suits chest and legs clamp over my body, my mask still open as I listen. "We made it back safely and landed, but as we disembarked I grabbed my two best men and we stole a transport and flew it back. I wasn't about to let my men die for nothing. Halfway there I get a call from command demanding I turn the ship around, so of course I tell them no and cut the call." His eyes break from mine as he stares off beside me, lost in his recollection. "Within moments they're on the line with my second in command, Major Ryar Gorthaine. They tell him I've been relieved of command and he is now the superior officer onboard and to apprehend me and turn the ship around. You know, I never thought my own men would turn on me so quickly but the little fucker did it. I nearly had him but Lieutenant Borowitz swept my legs." He looks back into my eyes. "They stripped me of all ranks, gutted my suit, and sentenced me to wait out the rest of the war in a prison cell." He stops and stares at me as if to say *that's it* as I step forward and lift my hand and place it on his shoulder as he looks up at me.

"I would have done the same for my men," I say encouragingly as I rock him a bit with my hand. "I would die in the defense of any human; it's the oath we take as cervos. And I would especially do it for my herd. Now let's go make sure these kids get home safe," I finish as I walk past him and let my suit's mask close. He follows behind as we leave the workshop in silence.

I immediately see notifications from both Majors Pirez and Thorne as my mask's heads-up display begins its rendering procedures. Thorne's message simply states the readiness of our defenses but Pirez's is a link to the short-range scanners. I pull the readings up to the bottom left of my HUD and see thousands of small dots approaching and a small counter beneath stating two hours and thirty-seven minutes till atmospheric breach. I've read the scanners a thousand times but I've never seen anything like this. Using my suit's integrated haptic glove I open a comms link with Pirez.

"Major, what is it I'm looking at here?" I ask bluntly with a hint of confusion.

"The tip of the spear, sir," she says with a shiver of fear on her voice. "Based on calculations from the size of the sonar scans and what we've seen so far, we could be looking at some seven-thousand ships," she says, again in the same tone.

"That's three times the size of Bilemy," I say in a flat tone. "Is there any good news from the scans?" I ask with false hope as sweat already begins to drip from my brow.

"The majority appear to be fighter and transport class, sir; crews could range anywhere from four to forty. No outward communications signals so far, and no long-range firing capabilities from what we can tell and most are spewing high vapor trails, which is a sign of fuel leaks or being nearly derelict. These are indeed junkers, sir. They're so beat up that a few shots may take them down and I think this will buy us more time than we thought. I suspect that if they breach the atmosphere they most likely won't be able to leave it again," she states with a glint of hope, yet my mind whirls at the question of who these people are. *This is an invasion like never before seen.'*

"Focus fire on the larger transports and inform Welsh and Mackie to begin prepping for ion volleys. I want one every eight minutes once this starts, understood?" I order to her as I walk down the halls of the now dim and quiet bunkhouses with Fawkes beside me.

"Crystal clear, sir, prepping the ion cannon now," she states as her comm link ends and I open a new link with Fawkes and relay my new information.

"Who could they possibly be? This doesn't look like serfs," I ask him as we walk amongst the dull blue emergency lights.

"I don't know but it reminds me of *The Volk*," he says absentmindedly as we exit the bunk area and into the vast maze of barricades.

"The Volk?" I question back as I ponder the word he used.

"Might have been called something else where you're from. As a kid, my ma always told me stories of space adventurers and pioneers that went too far into the void and lost their minds, and if I wasn't a good boy they would come down at night and steal me to peel my skin off," he says with a reminiscent voice.

"Your mother sounds delightful," I laugh over the comms.

"Kept me in line," he laughs back.

"My uncle called them flayers," I state after the laughter dies.

"Volk, flayer, serf. I don't care who they are, they killed my crew," he says, bolstering himself as we cross the threshold into the atrium.

Chapter 12

A Question of Loyalty

The atrium is busy with activity when we enter. Barricades have been placed to section off half of the large room from the base of the stairs creating a long wall of defenses pointed directly at the steel double doors of the facility. I walk up the left staircase to the landing where I see Major Thorne overseeing the operation. He stands next to a manned mini-gun placed where I gave my speech only hours ago. He sees me ascending as he turns.

"Commander, the defenses have been set and we are awaiting further commands." He salutes as I stand before him, his posture showing his readiness and bravery.

"Excellent, Major. I'll be at the second checkpoint in the command center with the secondary force observing the situation through the cameras. If I give the retreat order, I want all non-cervo units out first, with you and the herd holding the rear, understood?" I order as I look around and see a well-placed and manned defensive position.

"Right, sir." He nods. "Permission to speak freely?" He stands at attention as he asks.

"Of course, Major," I offer without repose. As my second in command, I trust his word over any others.

"What if these junkers are just a meat shield? What if the real force is still beyond our scanners?" he questions with good reason as he looks me in the eyes with an unwavering stare.

"That's a fair assumption, Major. It very well could be. But we don't know and that's not a variable I can accept to make me change my orders. The belt will focus on the transport ships before too many land and the belt is overwhelmed. Your question is fair and noted. Is there anything else?" I ask, his words well thought and spoken.

"Actually, sir, if I may?" he says as I see a private comm link request from him. I acknowledge the request as he begins to speak directly into my suit from his. "Are you sure we can trust this guy?" he asks as his head slightly nods towards Fawkes.

"Why shouldn't we? His information has been solid thus far," I retort as I'm taken aback by this sudden accusation.

"But, what if he's just a scout? What if these guys stole that ship from EIC and used it as a ruse to see our defensive state?" he continues with a genuine tone of concern.

"Adrian, you saw the crash site personally. If it was a ruse, why not just land the ship? Why risk losing every person onboard and destroying a perfectly good recon ship?" I question back.

"I'm not sure, sir, something just doesn't feel right about it," he says with a lack of justification.

"Fawkes was on Bilemy. He was the leader of the team that found the Crissium stronghold and he risked everything to bring his men home. I know he was a prisoner only hours ago, but dammit, he's a cervo and I trust him and you should too, Major," I state, getting slightly irritated.

"But, sir—" he tries to continue as I cut him off.

"No *buts*, Adrian, I trust him as much as I trusted you and the herd to hold that door on Arili next to me and that should be enough for you. We need every fighting man and woman we can get. Now is there anything else or would you like accuse another member of our crew of being a turncoat?" I ask as I finish my statement.

"None, sir," he says as he salutes, keeping his composure, though I can tell he didn't enjoy being chewed out by me.

"Thank you, Major, now be ready for anything," I say and nod as I ascend the main staircase and head for the command center, Fawkes following in silence.

I can't help but smirk behind my mask at the thought of what a great soldier Thorne has become over the years. He was eighteen when a planetary conscription forced him to join the service; he was a cadet when he was dropped on Arili with nineteen others. He was a reckless kid. I could barely get him to follow orders when he was put under my command. I always had a fondness for breaking soldiers with the *screw this* attitude; it was sink or swim under my command back then. I'd send him on monotonous errands, give him back-to-back guard shifts and even make him recite the cadet's handbook from start to finish. It took some time but he finally started to show real change about three years in after we came upon an earth-loyal town that had been attacked by a large serf force. The bodies were piled in the streets which was common for the serfs and not an uncommon sight for us. Beds and mattresses were scattered and on each of them were the bodies of women. It was clear what the serfs had done but did they have to do it to the children too? What kind of monster could call that freedom from oppression? Thorne threw his helmet off and cried like a child, sobbing into his metal hands. He personally took charge to ensure all the bodies were laid to rest. I offered him the Lieutenant's position shortly after and he has been an unwavering soldier of Earth since.

I walk briskly with Fawkes through the halls to the command center, its once wide and long halls now filled with multi-leveled barricades and shielded defensive positions. I make sure to nod or salute to every soldier I see, and I can see the fear in their eyes. I've felt that very same fear more than once. It fades with experience. Most have never seen me in my C-suit as their eyes widen seeing the commander's emblem emblazoned on the shoulders. I tap the access panel for the command center and the steel shutter door slides up and opens to the bustling command center. Two armored cervo units stand guard at the door as I approach.

"Officer on deck!" both Hector and Drake yell in unison through their suits' speakers as everyone comes to a sudden halt and turns to salute. I motion them back to their positions as I step in with extra heavy footsteps, more for effect as I already have control of the room and walk slowly to my terminal overlooking everyone else as I let my mask slide open. I look into the faces of each man and woman as I toggle my comms to the entire station.

"Soldiers of Whitman Station, today we face an enemy we may have never seen before. They have no outward communication and they have shot down an EIC class ship. We must therefore assume them to be hostile. As we speak, this massive fleet of ships is descending upon us, and within a few minutes Major Pirez will initiate a rail gun salvo on the fleet. We will not shoot all of them down and this will most likely end with a land assault on the station. We have just two hours before they breach the atmosphere, at which point we will have roughly thirteen hours to defend the station before the upload is complete and we can call for help." I pause, seeing my words fall on the soldiers before me with dread. "But all is not lost, for we are soldiers of Earth. We made an oath to our home and our ancestors. We will protect Earth and all of its posterity. Today I ask you all to put your lives on the line for every man, woman, and child across the cosmos. We are cervos, we are soldiers, we are Earth. Thank you, Whitman Station." I end my speech and cut the comm link, leaving an open line with Pirez as I see the nodding heads of my soldiers and the resolve growing in their eyes.

"The belt is ready and technicians are on standby, sir," Pirez states with readiness.

"Major Pirez, initiate the fire of the gun belt," I order in a calm and robust voice.

"Opening fire now, sir," she replies back with confidence.

Within moments we all hear the gun belt whirl to life. From inside it sounds like fireworks going off as the short-range scanners show ships popping off the screen dozens at a time. Several minutes pass as I see some fifteen hundred ships removed from the scanner screens, two thousand, twenty-five hundred, then silence. Soon a walloping sound of energy hurtles into the distant skies as the ion cannon activates, tearing long lines through the images on the scanners. There are cheers all around the command center as the soldiers see the devastation our weapons can achieve. I continue to watch the monitors as I think more about these junker ships and how they must not have many capabilities.

"Donovan," I shout from my terminal. "Have the scanners picked up any antigravity signals from those ships?" I ask as he looks up towards me in acknowledgment then back down and toggles his terminal's keyboard for a few seconds.

"Nothing on the short-range, sir. Few ships of such a small size are outfitted with antigravity and based off the state of these ships, it's highly unlikely they have anti-gravity," he yells up to me from his chair.

"Then they may not be used to gravity. Just to be safe I'd like you to slightly increase the gravity generator on the station by a few points," I say as his eyebrow arches in a questioning manner. "Nothing more than we are used to, but it may have a greater effect on them," I say with a wise tone.

"The increase will take effect momentarily, Commander," he says with a hurried voice as he taps his keyboard.

I take a moment to update every one of the incoming gravity spike and within a few minutes I can feel a few more pounds of weight fall on my already tired shoulders. The crackling sound of the gun belt continues as everyone adjusts to the new shifting weights. The scanners fill with more ships from the edge of the range as the forward section falls to pieces under the might of the precision blasts, the ion cannon tearing massive holes through their ranks every eight minutes. Fifteen more ion rounds follow over the next two hours as the sparingly fired rail guns slow to a halt as each gun empties its ammunition into the descending enemy. Seeing dozens more ships entering range as they grow closer and closer to the atmosphere, I see a comms request from Pirez pop up on my display.

"Update," I order as I open the link to her.

"All rounds fired, sir. We approximate almost three thousand destroyed or wounded enough that they'll burn up upon atmospheric entry," she says in a proud tone of voice as she just managed to take nine minutes of ammunition and spread it across two hours.

"Very good work, Major Pirez. Please allocate your gun technicians to the defensive position outside of the engineering command center," I order, knowing this is only the calm before the storm.

"Already in position, sir," she retorts and ends her comm link and I turn from my terminal, seeing Fawkes standing at attention behind me. I can see heavy beads of sweat pouring across his brow.

"Are you all right, Fawkes?" I ask as he wipes the sweat away with his metal forearm, when I hear a robotic voice shouting at the cervos guarding the door. I look over and see Dr. Vyers arguing with Drake as I turn and approach. "Dr. Vyers, what brings you to command? You should be in your triage."

"Yes, I very well should," she says in a sarcastic tone as she pulls her hand up, showing two large syringes in it. "These are stimulant injections for both you and Mr. Fawkes. It has been a long time for the both of you and you'll need these to stay focused. Normally I would send my droids for such a menial task, but as you know—" I hold my hand up to stop her before she begins to rant.

"Thank you, Claire," I say in a professional tone as I take the two syringes from her. "Now please, for your safety, I'd like you to return to medical and await further order, understood?" She looks at me with tears building in her eyes as she nods affirmative and turns from the command center back to her medical bay.

I turn to Fawkes and hand him the syringe as I activate a small injection tube from the left forearm of my suit and inject the stimulant. Within seconds I feel a rush of adrenaline and pain relief as the weight on my shoulders subsides. I see Fawkes do the same as a wave of easement washes over his face. He nods, looking at me and shuffles in place letting the stimulant do its job. I nod back and return to my terminal. Glaring at the screen, I can see the ten camera feeds from the atrium, twelve from the exterior and four from engineering. From the atrium I see soldiers shuffling in place clearly riddled with anxiousness. Engineering is busy with technicians at their terminals, and the exterior is dead quiet. I look to the short-range scanners once more and see the first few ships break the atmosphere as our local scanners begin picking up signals.

"We have atmospheric breach. Company will arrive in twelve minutes," I say into the PA system to the entire crew.

Chapter 13

When the Levee Breaks

I watch as the seconds tick by on the monitor. Still twelve hours and forty-three minutes to go until the upload is complete. The white blips growing closer and closer as our local scanners and exterior cameras begin to pick up ships touching down about a half a klick surrounding the facility on all sides. I tap the button on my terminal to open the observation windows inlaid into the ceiling. Everybody looks up as the solar blinds open and slide away, revealing an open blue sky massed with a swarm of ships descending around us like angry insects. Some fly close enough that I can see the scorch marks of previous battles and varying states of disrepair as I can tell these ships are indeed junkers and I'm surprised they even function. Within seconds I'm pulled from my observations and close the solar blinds as the droids outside begin to feed us information.

"Donovan, what are we seeing here?" I order as numbers and colors flash across the screen in a blur as they pick up many entities outside.

"Droids one and two are picking up dozens of heartbeats. Droid three overlooking the practice yard has nothing yet, sir. Counting at least three hundred now and growing," he yells from his terminal.

I look down, trying to make some sense of the scans as suddenly droid one loses its connection. Within seconds droid two disconnects as well.

"Donovan?" I ask from my terminal in a confused tone.

"Both are gone, sir," he continues but is cut off as droid three goes down. "But there wasn't even proximity readings!" he yells at his terminal screen. "I don't know how the last one went down, sir." He throws his hands up as he yells from his seat, clearly confused as to how we lost the third droid.

"Could be a sniper," I say as from around the facility I hear what sounds like firecrackers going off outside.

"Auto turrets have activated, sir. There are hostiles on the perimeter," Corporal Skyes yells from her station as several more turrets activate. "A lot of hostiles, sir."

I bring my attention to the exterior camera feeds and soon I see figures in the distance, first only a dozen then suddenly a hundred as they mass near the far end of the entrance to the station grounds. They are a rabble of mostly men but some women are present. They are disheveled and dirty. They run as a massive horde towards the station as I can see outdated weaponry, some wielding homemade swords twice the size of themselves. Fragmented pieces of steel plate armor swinging from ropes are knotted over open pale skin and tattered fabric clothing. I zoom in on their faces and see people clearly sick from vacuum exposure, dark blue war paint plastered across every one of them in swirls and unknown insignias. Their hair is fashioned into high pointed styles or shaved into menacing mohawks. The image reminds me of the *Picts* from ancient Scotland, a race so fearsome, brutal and unruly that they terrified the Romans so much they simply built a wall to keep them away from their colonies. They dash for the main doors of the station. Soon a pile of bodies lies across the main strip leading up to the doors as the auto turrets cut down any closest target. Soon the sound of firecrackers grows lower as archaic ballistic guns shoot out the turret systems one by one. Some throw improvised grenades against the turrets causing small shakes around the station as they explode in a flash of smoke and concussive force causing several structural damage reports to flare up across my terminals screen.

"Turret systems are going offline all around the station, sir," Corporal Skyes says softly from her station as I click my comm to Major Thorne.

"Adrian, they'll be at the door in three minutes. Good luck, Major," I say into my suit's speaker.

"You too, sir. All for Earth," he says calmly as the horde smashes itself against the steel doors.

"All for Earth," I reply and nod.

Soon our exterior cameras blink off one after another, their last images showing guns aiming towards them as they leave us blind to anything else that could be coming. I switch my terminal to the atrium's camera feeds and watch as I see Major Thorne shouting orders to the troops as they ready their guns and kneel behind their barricades. A soft yellow glow of heating metal becomes visible on the door as it slowly grows bigger and brighter. Almost thirty minutes pass as the door begins to sag and give out. A large section of the door suddenly bursts in and falls to the ground with a heavy smack as through the hole comes pouring these marauders. They flood in like water through a broken dam. Bodies fall rapidly as they are blasted with volleys of rail-rifle fire; they scream like banshees as they charge through the molten-rimmed hole. First thing I notice is how sluggish they are as they climb over the bodies of their own fallen. *'I knew they wouldn't like the gravity here.'* I smirk as I watch the horde clamor over the dead, still barely ten meters from the barricades as suddenly two black orbs arc across the room and land behind the defenses on the right flank. A blast wave of smoke and fire erupts amongst the soldiers as the grenades explode, sending troops flying in all directions. With the right flank compromised the horde pushes closer then up and over the barricade as I see a few cervo units step in front of the regular soldiers, their heavy metal hands denting armor and breaking bones as they engage the enemy. I see the cervos on the right flank get overwhelmed quickly as I tap into Major Thorne's comms.

"Start pulling back, Adrian!" I order briskly.

"We can hold, sir!" he shouts over screaming and rifle fire.

"Your flank is compromised, Major, I won't lose half the unit to the first defense. Pull back to secondary now! This is a direct order, Major, please comply!" I demand.

"Understood, sir," he says with a tinge of reluctance.

As I cut comms I can see him through the camera feed giving the retreat order. I view as the soldiers pull back one by one as the cervos hold the left flank and the landing where the mini-gun is, its steel barrels red hot with unending use. Bodies are strewn across the main atrium floor; some are my men but easily one hundred or more are that of the enemy. I see as the last of the soldiers move up the main stairs heading for the barricaded hallways between here and the atrium, the cervos fight so savagely the enemy is almost avoiding them until a figure approaches through the molten hole into the doorway. He's big and covered in armor from head to toe. Something about him looks strangely familiar.

"What the hell is that, sir?" Donovan asks from his terminal as a wave of shocked gasps crosses the command center.

I zoom the camera in on the figure to get a better look as he steps into the atrium. His armor is bulky and solid black. Zooming in on the face I see a solid tinted glass facemask and a clear set of antlers along the sides of the head.

"It's a goddamn cervo!" I shout out loud as I pull the comms up to every cervo down there. "Herd, do not engage that thing! Pull back to secondary now!" I hear several affirmatives over the speakers but three units decide to disregard my order as they move forward like a pack of stalking wolves.

One approaches from the front as two attempt to circle around using pack tactics. I can't believe my eyes as I see he has almost two feet on my units. The titan simply stands in his pitch black patchwork of a cervo suit. As the cervos engage he quickly draws a massive black warpick from across his back and buries it through the facemask of the cervo in front of him. A pin drop could be heard in the command center as I see the soldier go limp and fall dead on the ground.

"Thorne! Get those men out of there. We need to close the upper doors now!" I demand, yelling into my speakers, but it's too late as the massive figure swings his pick and takes the leg off a cervo from the knee and finishes him with a downward swing to the neck as the soldier falls to the ground.

"Working on it now, sir!" Thorne yells as he turns from the top of the main staircase and descends to the platform next to the overheated mini-gun, activates his hooves and leaps off towards the beast.

Landing with a heavy thud, Thorne barrels towards the monstrosity as it grabs the remaining cervo by the throat and feeds shots to his faceplate with its solid gauntlets until his mask cracks and breaks as streaks of blood can be seen flying off its fist with each swing. His body crumples to the floor as Thorne activates a burst from his hooves and dashes towards the black-clad titan and spears him from the waist, throwing both of them off balance and into the wall. The beast pushes Thorne from him and swings his oversized fists as Thorne ducks low and counters with an uppercut to the jaw, The beast's head barely moves upon contact. The hooves of the titan glow with activation as it attempts to kick up to Thorne's chest, but Thorne is faster as he kicks the hoof down into the ground as the blast goes off and concrete dust billows out around both of them. The beast lets out a blood-curdling roar as it brings both fists up and hammers them both down on Thorne's shoulders, causing him to sway off balance as the titan wraps his massive hands around Thorne's helmet and make a quick jerking motion as Thorne's helmet turns completely around and his body drops to the floor.

"Adrian!" I scream and smash my fist into the housing of my terminal as I hear audible shrieks come from some of my technicians. "I want everyone to pull back now, goddammit!" I shout with a cracking voice across the comm channels as I use all my power to hold back tears.

I see through tear-blurred vision as the flood of enemies take the room as the security door slides shut, several of them smashing their weapons against it in anger and pure rage. *'I said pull back, you idiot. Pull back means fucking pull back!'* I smash my metal fist against the housing of my terminal again, this time leaving a dent in the metal and a large crack appears across the thick glass screen.

"Commander, what do we do now?" Lieutenant Spurs questions with concern as his voice comes in over my speakers. *'Death happens but the battle isn't over. Don't let this consume you,'* I repeat to myself as Spurs calls again "Commander!" he shouts, breaking me from my lost focus.

"Spurs, you're in command of the frontline now. I'm promoting you to Major and I want you to reposition with the herd up front and the soldiers in the back," I order, giving him a battlefield promotion as I watch the camera feed from the atrium. "They're hauling a plasma cutter in; they'll be through that door in about a half an hour, so be ready, Major," I say and watch the black colossus lord over his victory as his army floods in around him like a rock splitting the flow of a raging river.

I watch as the tank begins to give hand signals to the savages around him. They shake their heads and one by one begin to shoot out every camera they can see, each feed going black until I see nothing but my reflection in the faded glass of my terminal, my eyes meeting that of my reflections. *'I'm gonna kill every last one of them,'* I think to myself as I close the dead camera feeds and turn to the dozens of damage reports flowing in from across the station. Concussion blasts and ballistic damage to the solar blinds have been ineffective so far, but the thick steel blinds won't hold forever.

"Spurs, did anyone get a good look at that thing?" I question with haste as heat signatures become present on the door to the second level.

"Negative, sir, it was a black mass... moved like a shadow..." he stammers as I can tell he too is feeling the loss of Major Thorne.

"Understood, just hold back and prepare yourselves for anything. This enemy is officially unpredictable. I don't want anybody engaging with that thing until we find a weak spot, is that understood, Major? If it engages again, I want you to pull back to the next checkpoint at the command center," I order with angst and wave my hand to get Donovan's attention. "Donovan, review the footage and get me any statistics you can on that thing. Everything has a weak point, we just have to find it," I command down to him from my position.

"Yes, sir," he replies with calm precision as he pulls up the security footage and any usable body cam footage from the herd and begins to take frames of the black beast and analyze them.

Minutes pass as I watch the camera feed from the hallway on the second floor. The door is glowing a bright yellow as small flashes of fire burst from it in wispy tongues. I reopen the observation port in the ceiling. Looking up through the thick glass I can see hundreds if not thousands more of these low-class ships skirting around the air like buzzards over their scraps. I feel a rumble and see another ion blast arc across the sky as it disintegrates most ships caught in its trajectory, others simply lose power and spiral to the ground at immense speeds.

"Anything yet, Donovan?" I ask, bringing my attention back to my surroundings.

"Not much, sir, if I can be honest. All I can tell from the footage is that this suit didn't come from any of our foundries; its shape doesn't match the molds of any manufacturer. This must have been built by a third party, sir," he shouts up to me from his terminal.

"Then we will have to find our own weak spot," I say out loud to myself.

Chapter 14

The Cordoba

The security doors only last a few more minutes as the metal sags and fall forward, enemies pouring in soon after the plasma cutter is pulled back and away from the glowing hole it made. The emergency door to the officer's wing is sealed, forcing the enemy to turn right and directly into the line of barricades only ten meters away, rail rifles rounds tearing through the first line of attackers as the mini-guns open fire on them. Bodies pile so high in the hall that some enemies throw grenades in to clear the way for more to charge towards the defenses, more running through covered in blood and screaming a horrid war cry.

Soon screams can be heard from the distance outside the command center, high-pitched yips and deep roaring bellows echoing down the hallways, reminding me of the *rebel yell* used by ancient American civil war rebels to frighten the enemy union soldiers. Cameras continue to fail one after the other, their final images showing the enemy taking the first line of barricades and running down any one of my soldiers that get too close to them. Suddenly I see a body cam link open up from Spurs. I accept and watch with horror as these things rip into my fleeing soldiers. Spurs orders a shield wall as he and six cervos stand side by side and magnetically lock themselves in place, claiming melee weapons from the enemies' hands and turning them against them. The position holds for some time as enemies fall to the power of the herd. With Spurs holding, I take a moment to call for an update from Major Pirez.

"It appears the entire fleet is in range now, Commander," she says clearly disheveled from the death of Major Thorne, but continues. "They've got what looks like a possible flagship and nine other larger vessels, perhaps command ships?" she questions as she updates me.

"Get me scans on all the ships and begin ion salvos targeting them specifically," I order as I look to the scanners and see nine cruiser-type class ships and a very large oval shaped ship with a large square protruding from each end.

I look up through the view port in the ceiling and can see the outline of the massive ship breaching the atmosphere. The others are there but barely visible at this distance. A few seconds later I can feel the low hum in the floor as the ion cannon revs up and fires. I see a long pinkish blast of energy sail skyward at impeccable speeds as it connects with one of the smaller cruisers and tears through any junkers in its path. It sears through the hull and the ship lights ablaze as it begins a descending freefall towards the ground; cheers come from several soldiers in the command center as we see it career downwards until it falls far beyond the horizon.

"Turn your attention to the flagship next!" I order as the scanners indicate the remaining eight smaller cruisers are redirecting their courses to behind the massive oval ship.

Eight minutes pass, giving the ion cannon time to cool down as another shot rockets out towards the colossal ship, clearly only some fifty klicks above us in the stratosphere. The shot arcs across the sky in mere seconds as moments before contact the ship whirls to life with a massive green shell of translucent energy that deflects the ion blast that soon disappears after the shot disperses.

"Shield tech? But how?" I hear come from Fawkes behind me.

"Not sure but we are gonna find out," I say as I toggle Pirez in the comms. "Sasha, have your scans picked up anything yet?" I order to her through my speaker.

"Nothing yet, sir, but we have a lot of background interference to sift through first. Shall I continue ion blasts?" she asks as I hear her keypad tapping over her mic.

"Affirmative. Even the shields of the best ships in our fleet can only withstand four or five of those." I click my comms off and turn my attention to the battle in the hallway. Reports are coming in that dozens are dead in the hall but the main force is still strong and holding. Cervos are engaging anyone close in melee as the soldiers provide cover fire and throw grenades. They're holding for now but some are beginning to waver. Eight more minutes pass as the ion cannon readies another volley, but this time the ion cannon springs to life and nothing happens as it misfires and lets loose nothing but a heavy sound of grinding gears. I watch from below as the green shield encases the ship for a brief moment then disappears again. Within seconds Pirez is calling me.

"Commander, they have an outdated shield generator – it looks like first generation tech – and with a recharge rate faster than the ion cannon, they could potentially take those blasts all day!" she yells from her terminal in the heart of Whitman Station.

'Recharge? That thing must be ancient,' I ponder to myself, looking again at the outline of the flagship on our scanners. Somehow I swear I know that ship. The shape, the shield generator, it all looks so familiar as I try to put the pieces together. Then suddenly my eyes widen as my brain makes the connection

that I have that very ship in scale model in my room.

"That's The Cordoba!" I say loud enough for everyone to hear as I yell to Spurs from the frontlines. "Make a hole, Major, I need to get to the officer's wing now!" I order as I unlock the officer's wing from my terminal and step away and motion for Fawkes, Hector and Drake to follow me. "Donovan, you have command until Spurs arrives," I shout as I walk towards the door and signal Spurs that we are in position.

"Stampede!" Spurs orders with a yell as the four of us stand at the far end of the entrance to the command center and prep our hooves.

The magnetic boots of my suit grip the ground and with a burst of energy we are leaping over the barricades in single bounds, soldiers ducking their heads as we soar over them. Each leap brings me closer to engagement as I feel a rush of memories flow in as I feel alive again. My suit lands amongst the rabble of enemies as muscle memory kicks in and my fists take action, breaking limbs with ease as these monsters attempt to surround me. A Spartan kick sends a savage back, toppling dozens and killing several as my fist finds the jaw of another and tears it off as it continues and makes contact with the chest of the one beside him, caving his rib cage in and stopping his heart in an instant. There is blood, viscera and limbs flying around the four of us as we push past the melted steel doors dividing the atrium from the hall; my scanners tell me there is twelve percent blood in the air. We rip through the enemy's advance in mere minutes as we make it past their numbers and leap down the hall in two leaps and come to the bend leading to the officer's wing, the enemy hot on our trail.

Chapter 15

The Paradigm Shift

"You two hold here!" I order and point at the corner. "We won't be long," I say, turning and leaping towards my room with Fawkes. Hector and Drake salute and pull their rail rifles from their backs and begin engaging the approaching enemy from the long distance of the hall, tossing several grenades before opening fire. The emergency lights glow in a soft blue as I hear their rifles open fire after a few small explosions with the sound of screams and bodies dropping soon follow.

Leaping in a few strides we find ourselves in the quiet officer's wing. All the doors have been locked down and all power cut except the emergency lighting. We arrive at my door as I activate my override code and the door slides up with the sound of shifting steel. My room is dark but exactly the way I left it. We enter and I make for my display wall where I see the hundred souvenirs I've collected through my service. I look to my model ships and tucked up in the right corner I see the 1:1000 scale model of the Cordoba. I snag it and turn to my bookshelf as I see Fawkes admiring my vast array of weaponry on the wall. I sift through the book titles when I come upon *The Unpredictable Frontier: Only Voyage of The Cordoba.* I pull the book down and on the cover I see a well-dressed and young admiral standing cross-armed in front of the massive oval ship.

"All right, got it, let's go," I say, turning to see Fawkes with my black glass war hammer gripped in both hands.

"Do you mind?" he asks, hoping he didn't offend.

"By all means, it was just collecting dust," I offer as I walk to the wall of weapons and reach for my most prized possession, the bastard sword given to me when I was decorated for my heroic work on Arili. Although swords are rarely in the military anymore, it is tradition to be gifted swords for acts of valor in the face of daring odds. I pull the sheath off with force and toss it to the ground as I hold the sword to my face. Engraved at the base above the hilt is the Earthling military insignia showing Earth with each terraformed planet orbiting around it and along the center of the blade itself is my name and the planet I was stationed on. The blade is made of titanium with a tungsten carbide edge; it's a long blade but very light as I swing it around a few times. I put the model and book in my suit's storage compartment located on the lower back as we both nod to each other and exit my room, locking the door behind us. Stepping out I hear close-range gun fire as both Hector and Drake come running around the corner, their armor scorched with bullet fire.

"We've lost the position, sir!" Drake says as Hector fires at the enemy around the corner, his rail rifle emptying as he drops it and pulls his pistol to return fire once more. I draw a pistol from my waist to my left hand and grip the sword in my right as I tell my suit through my implants to open comm links with both Pirez and Spurs.

"Updates now!" I bark as I peek my pistol around the corner and fire at the enemies running from about thirty meters away, each shot dropping a wretch in its tracks. Spurs being on the frontlines chimes in first over the link.

"Commander, we have a swarm here. We've lost at least fifty; four were cervos. That thing is unstoppable. We haven't found any way to hurt him thus far and we've lost a lot of ground," he yells over gun fire and screams.

"Maintain your ground for another ten meters then fall back into the command center; the doors to command are three times thicker than the main entrance so it should buy us some time. Pirez, report!" I order across the comm link as we exchange fire and plot an alternate route around the far end of the officer's wing.

"Ships are still making touch down, sir. We are overwhelmed. Some men are reporting sounds from above the railgun terminals; they could be cutting into the cable ducts, sir." As she is replying her update there is a sudden crash followed by screams. "They are in the rail hall, sir!" she screams over the commotion.

"Pull everyone back into central engineering, now, Sasha! Seal the doors to you and to the command center. We can't let Spurs and the main force get surrounded. Spurs, fall back now and consolidate, we need a minute to think." Both give affirmatives as I turn back to the battle at hand, firing my pistol's remaining shots as the enemy grows ever close. "Everyone pull back to my room!" I shout as I unlock the door, all four of us running in just as the enemy horde turns the corner charging towards us.

The door slides shut and seconds later there is a heavy smack of bodies hitting the other side, weapons clanging against the solid steel with low thuds. I motion to the wall of weapons. "Take whatever you like and gear up." All three peruse my collection and begin grabbing old firearms and melee weapons as I go to my desk and pull the book from my storage compartment. I open the table of contents and see *Shield Generator pg.121.* I flip to the page and begin reading. The Cordoba was built in the late end of the expansion some forty years ago; it was a glamorous time where money was spent frivolously on wild ideas. One of these grand ideas was to build a ship that could map the asteroid belts that are present in almost every system. Many would-be explorers and pioneers have lost their lives or minds to the vast fields of chaos. The man picked to captain the vessel was Admiral Samuel Kist, a young up and comer famous for his military exploits and naval accomplishments. The ship went missing some four years into journey and was simply reported lost in space as nothing could ever be found. *'Clearly not the case,'* I think to myself as I read more. It was equipped with the very first prototype shield generator, built to withstand an asteroid collision. Although ancient by today's standards, it requires a power-up period and can only be active for a few seconds before overheating. *"It needs three minutes!"* I shout to myself in my suit. I smile big and key the comms to my Majors.

"All right, time to shift the paradigm. We are going to pull a Scudinski on these guys!" Both give a shocked and confused reaction as I continue. "Just hear me out. Their shields need three minutes to recharge and if we fire a blank charge the machine won't warm up and we can fire a secondary blast in ninety seconds, not the usual eight minutes. We are going to make a long dash around the other side of the facility and come down on engineering, so Pirez I'm going to need you to unseal the ion booth as we approach," I plot as she cuts me off.

"Not possible, sir, these bastards are already starting to sever internal power links. It has to be done from the inside or from the outside access panel. Mackie and Welsh are in there now, but I'm getting no response from either," she reports with unease in her voice.

"Then hopefully the panel is still there. We are Oscar Mike

in one minute," I say as I gather up my men, all three now sporting a good portion of my collection. "All right herd, when I open that door I want to see the greatest stampede I've ever seen. I don't just mean run fast; we need to get to the ion cannon. I wanna see clear disregard of military property." I give each one a push on the shoulder as they grind their hooves like elk about to clash antlers and make deep gouges in the floor. "I wanna see you tear these fucking walls down on these assholes! This is our home, and I'd rather bring it down than let them have it! Do you fucking hear me?" I cry behind my mask. I've never felt so goddamn alive as we all stamp our feet and they line up in single file behind me, Fawkes holding the rear.

I toggle the command to open the door. As the steel slides open, several enemies fall to the ground on each other. I trigger my suit's magnetic hooves and blast through the door at sixty kilometers an hour; anyone in the doorway is eviscerated as I charge through them. Bodies blast against the walls as eight heavy hooves send shockwaves into the ground. Some don't stand back up. I leap up with another thrust of my boot and as I come down I see a group separate to avoid my heavy landing. One isn't so lucky as he trips and my boot lands on his shoulder and pulses again, sending his bottom half flying as the rest of him washes over me. Up ahead I see a right turn. Beside me running along the wall in great leaps is Hector. He dashes ahead and thrusts against the far-left wall, propelling himself down the right turn. The three of us follow in unison.

As I leap around the corner my foot doesn't plant properly and throws me off balance as I tilt sideways and smash into the wall, crushing several enemies. I hear gun fire and melee combat as I collect myself and stand, pulling up my sharp titanium blade. I spin it around me, severing arteries and cutting limbs like they are soft cheese. I get lost in the fray as each savage I cut down is replaced with two others. I look and see Fawkes swing his war hammer against the head of a man which erupts in a splash of red. I attempt to fight my way to him as I see an enemy come up behind him with some sort of homemade shotgun. He lets loose five or six rounds in an automatic succession before I grab him by the throat and squeeze with my twenty-thousand psi robotic hand, his windpipe collapsing in my grip.

I turn to take a defensive stance when a heavy metal fist connects with my chest plate and throws me back several meters, knocking me prone. Looking up I see the black-clad titan looming before us amongst the rabble of savages. Before I can stand the beast lifts his hoof towards me. I can see the three magnetic reservoirs powering up with their blue metallic glow. Before I can even take another breath, a small burst of pistol rounds fire into the housing of the massive hoof. Several shots connect as the three rings power down and begin to spark. The black colossus looks over me to see Hector firing down on him. Forgetting me on the ground the beast jumps over me towards Hector as they enter an exchange of fists. Within seconds the behemoth has Hector pinned by the throat against the wall, feeding shots to his visor. He cocks back his arm for another heavy punch as Drake pulses with his boots and grabs the titan by his elbow, swinging him off balance and releasing Hector. The three of them exchange a few more punches and kicks as Hector calls me over the comms.

"Get to the ion cannon! Go!" Hector yells as he ducks to avoid an incoming fist and counters with an uppercut to the heavy jaw of the beast. "We will hold him back, sir!" He winces as a roundhouse kick connects with his waist.

"Hold him back? He's going to slaughter you!" I yell as my

sword cuts down three savages in front of me as I try to make may way to them. "I'm not leaving my men behind to die!" I scream as my sword buries into the unprotected skull of another savage.

"Fawkes! Get the Commander out of here!" Drake screams as he runs and tackles the beast at the waist, throwing him off balance as Hector thrusts with his boots and forces the beast prone.

In the span of a heartbeat the behemoth flips onto his back and sweeps Hector's legs, forcing him to the ground, his black metal gauntlet wrapping around Hector's neck and squeezing. The mass of the rabble around them forces Drake back to engage them as Hector's comm link severs and he begins to waver with his swings.

"Haves, we need to go now!" Fawkes yells as he pulls me from the shoulder in the other direction.

I begrudgingly nod to him and begin pushing against the enemies in our way, my sword-swings keeping them at a distance as they see their brethren cut down before me. I take a heavy stance and activate my hooves for a leap down the hall, taking a quick look back to see the beast stand and engage with Drake. They exchange shots but soon I lose them to the flood of enemies between us as I turn the corner with Fawkes and make for one of the stairwells to engineering.

Chapter 16

The Scudinski

I arrive with Fawkes at a stairwell on the other side of the station that leads down to engineering. I toggle the commander's override code and the door soon shifts open. I lock the door behind us as we bypass the three levels of stairs and leap down from landing to landing as we bend steel and crush concrete to dust with each jump until we reach the bottom. It's quiet here as we stand outside the sealed door to engineering. I once again toggle my override code on my HUD. Fawkes and I nod as I let the door slide into the ceiling. In front of us we see the hall is packed with these mongrels and some sort of hacker team is on their knees in front of us. Their smiles turn to fear as they see it wasn't them that had opened the door. One is met with a solid fist to the face as others receive a sword slash across their arms and chests. They drop in an instant as the entire hall goes quiet for a brief moment as all the enemies stare at us.

I charge with my sword and leap down on the savages, a blast wave of force throwing them away as I grab one by the head and smash him against the wall. I follow through with a sword slash across one's face, severing his head from the nose up as I barrel through with all my might. I land amongst them as a larger monster of a savage gets a lucky swing with a mallet to my face plate. I stand and take the hit without issue and return favor by grabbing his wrist and pulling his arm off. I take his mallet from his dead hand and throw it down the hall. As it lands dead center into another one's chest, she falls back, clutching at her deflated ribcage for a moment, then dies. Suddenly a small metal orb flies into the air and arcs, landing at my feet. My reflexes activate as I kick the grenade back towards the enemy causing it to land between a small group, the explosive burst sending pieces of the horde into the air. I push through the mass and run around the corner at immense speed and see a large swarm about twenty meters away running towards us. Fawkes stops next to me as we take a defensive stance.

"Are you familiar with the Dragon's Maw?" I ask him over the comms.

"Absolutely," he states with enthusiasm as I hear his right boot lock into place with its magnet.

"Perfect," I mutter as I do the same with my right foot. "Three." We pivot in unison, putting our left sides to the enemy. "Two." We both bring our left legs up, the soles of our hooves level with the enemy only five meters away. "One." We both scale a maxed-out magnetic shockwave into our left boots and release it as the enemy reaches one meter. The blast liquefies the first few dozen but the shockwave knocks down nearly the entire swarm of them. I disengage my magnetic grip and dash over the bewildered savages towards the door into the rail gun terminal hall as the few living enemies left standing flee from us in all directions.

I arrive in the rail hall as Fawkes keeps pace behind me. The place is swarmed with these things as we see them tearing at the electronics in the walls and scraping the terminals, but the more horrendous thing is what they are doing with the dead. They have strung them up from their feet and are cutting them apart like hunted game, carving filets and roasts from my dead soldiers and even their own fallen. My stomach sours as I grind my teeth. They look up, surprised as we engage the closest grouping. I approach as one pulls an old handgun and takes aim at me; a simple sword swing takes her hand off from the wrist as another takes her knees. My hand buries another's head into a terminal, the broken glass grinding into their face as they scream until my hand gives them release with a crunch to their spinal column. I make for the ion booth down the hall as a man in worn cotton clothes runs towards me with a bat. I kick his knee backwards and charge past him. I see Fawkes leap up and come down on a group with his hammer. My sensors tell me there is now fourteen percent blood in the air as a shockwave full of human parts paints the walls of the hallway and our C-suits.

A few leaps from the door to the ion room. I can see a team of hackers trying to get into the booth. I build up speed and barrel into one from behind and smear him against the door. My sword takes one from the waist as my knee thrusts another against the wall, crippling him. I pull and sever a mass of cables they had hooked up to the access panel in hopes of hacking the door; sparks fly out from the frayed ends as I toss it to the ground but the access panel is fried as I try to open the door. I toggle my override from my HUD and force the door open. As Fawkes and I lunge into the open doorway, it seals behind us as the clamor of weapons beats against it like a horrid rhythmic drumbeat.

I look around the large room as its terminals and displays beep and sound off with emergency sirens. I step towards the firing terminal and behind a desk I find the bodies of Lieutenant Mackie and Corporal Welsh, hands held together in a sad tableau as they lie motionless in their own blood with a pistol on the ground not far from them.

"Poor girls must have thought no one was coming when the

rail hall fell," Fawkes says as he lets his mask open and kneels down to close their eyes.

"Fear is a powerful thing," I state as I pick up the pistol they used and hold it in my hands. I clench it and put it in my holster as I turn to the monitors. I activate a systems check from the monitor as I open a link with the Majors. "We're in. Welsh and Mackie didn't make it," I state calmly as my eyes dance over the controls and the upload timer, still another eight hours left.

"They will be missed, sir," Pirez states with a solemn voice. "The cannon is ready and waiting to be loaded, Commander," she says, not letting the news halt her from her duties.

"Status on the door, Spurs?" I bark as I initiate the blank fire procedure from the terminal.

"We have maybe ten minutes before they burn through, sir! They've brought that damn plasma cutter up here with them," he says from the crowded command center.

"The halls between central on engineering are packed with hostiles. After we fire this salvo, I want the doors to both engineering and central to open and we can surround this swarm. Once they are cleared, we retreat to the hangar through engineering, understood?" Both give affirmatives as I focus on the task at hand.

I turn from the console and grab a steel s-hook from the wall and walk to the ion charges stacked along the right wall of the twenty-meter room, Fawkes following as I motion him without talking.

"So, what's a Scudinski?" he asks as he helps me drag a blank charge across the room to the loading system, the rectangular charge being about three feet high and two feet around on each side.

"Corporal Ben Scudinski was a smart kid but really unlucky.

Placement rotation put him here in the ion booth by himself," I say, getting halfway across the room, the charge sliding behind us. "One morning he was asked to do a blank fire like we are now. The machine takes ninety seconds to fire after activation. From the camera feed we later watched, we saw him activate the procedure and then noticed he failed to load a blank charge. Startled at the realization, he grabbed a hook and started dragging the canister over." I point to the yellow box painted on the ground where the charge should be placed. "Scud walked backwards and ended up stepping into the loading square as the machine activated and it grabbed him instead," I say, placing the charge and pointing up. "The machine's loader grabber him and shot him up there." I point up at the two-foot-by-two-foot open square in the ceiling to the firing mechanism. "It squeezed him through the hole and tore his arms off then buried a six-inch firing pin into his right cheekbone," I continue as I walk to the activation terminal. "We could never get the cannon back to full efficiency after that, so let's hope this works because we literally have one shot at this," I say as the machine hums to life and a pair of robotic hands grab the charge and raise it up at thirty kilometers an hour through the loading hole and into the cannon.

The ion cannon makes noises as it begins its firing procedures. I watch intently from the scanners and see the Cordoba activate its shields in preparation. A brief moment passes and it looks like the machine misfired again as the shields deactivate around the massive oval ship. With my heart racing I activate a real firing procedure as I dash to the right wall and snag one of the few ion charges remaining, Fawkes helping me move it into place. Seconds pass as the pneumatic arms grab the charge and send it into the machine. In the span of a heartbeat the cannon takes it shot. *'Come on, you sonofabitch!'* Beads of sweat pour down my face as the scanners show a bright streak of energy blast towards the ship and make contact, tearing a hole through a quarter of its hull and scorching much of the ship. I can hear the cheers across the comm lines as we see the ship bow and teeter on its axis. Minutes pass as we see it begin to shift direction and turn away from the surface, the eight cruisers behind it doing the same along with any fighters still in the air.

"We did it!" Fawkes cheers as he grabs my shoulders from behind.

"They are retreating! A perfect shot, Commander!" I hear Pirez yell from the engineering command center.

"Not down here, they aren't. We don't have much time before the door fails, sir!" Spurs cuts in, the sound of sagging metal present over his voice.

"Spurs, open the retreating door and seal it behind you! We've got them surrounded. I'll give the signal soon," I order as I turn to Fawkes, his face drenched with sweat as he stands there with his mask open. "Ready to win this?" I ask, picking up his hammer and offering it to him.

"Let's fucking do it, Haves," he says, taking the hammer with gusto and letting his mask swing shut as we both turn to the door.

"No guts, no glory! Open the doors now!" I yell as I toggle the door to open as we leap out over a mass of enemy savages. From both ends I see the doors shift open as my remaining soldiers pour in around them from both sides.

Rifle fire and screams echo in the metal halls as the several dozen savages find themselves surrounded, their eyes darting from each side as they see their deaths inching closer in massive metal hooves. Cervos jump into the fray in pairs, leaping from wall to wall as they land down amongst the enemy as rifle fire helps clear a path for them to advance. The morale of the enemy breaks almost instantly as they make mad dashes for the holes carved into the cable ducts, fear plastered over their blue war paint as they struggle over each other for safety. I see cervos leap to the walls and tear the enemy down with the unmatchable grips of their black glass steel hands. From the left I can see Pirez with her engineering team pepper down a group attempting to charge them, as from the right I hear Spurs order a stampede. Four units including himself rear up and dash across the floor towards my position, bodies falling in all directions in the wake of their magnetic pulses. My sword shines red as I parry an attack and take an enemy's arm off from the shoulder. I turn and see the horde defeated and take a small breath of relief. *'Just a battle not the war, stay focused,'* I remind myself.

"Commander! The door!" Pirez shouts, pointing at the far door to the command center, its doors almost white hot as the plasma cutter melts through it.

"Retreat to the hangar! Spurs, take point!" I shout, being pulled from my moment of respite.

Every last soldier begins running through the door to the engineering command center, the remaining cervos holding the front and center of our ranks as Fawkes and I follow in last. I turn for a brief moment to seal the door behind us and as I look back I see the molten metal door sag and give way as enemies pour in from forty meters away. Amongst the rabble of blue war paint and outdated battle gear I see the towering black figure stand out amongst them. I can't see his face but I know he is looking at me. Fawkes shoots his hand up and gives a wave that quickly turns into a flip-off towards the black monstrosity, the door sealing in front of us seconds later.

Chapter 17

Expeditious Retreat

Boots thud against the ground in a descending trickle through the emergency tunnel to the hangar. I can hear the heavy breathing of my soldiers as we exit the small tunnel into the cavernous hangar. I look around at the staggered groups of personnel trying to take stock of our numbers. One soldier is on the ground with a large slash across his stomach. Two cervos attempt to treat him but his face soon grows pale and his cries for help cease.

"How many made it?" I ask to Pirez and Spurs as I approach them and let my mask swing open.

"Forty-three and thirteen cervos, including myself, Fawkes and you, sir," Spurs says with a sad tone.

"So few," Pirez says as her eyes tear up. *'I honestly thought there'd be less.'*

"They made the ultimate sacrifice, Sasha. Earth will remember them for it. We all will," I say, almost putting my heavy blood-crusted gauntlet on her shoulder. "How much longer till the upload finishes?" I ask, trying to get her to focus.

"Seven hours and thirty-four minutes, sir," she says, reading from her haptic glove.

"Then we hold till then. Those blast doors are the strongest our military can make," I say as I point up to the massive seventeen-foot thick steel hangar doors that make up the ceiling. "Those too." I point towards the door we came through. "Has anyone had contact with Dr. Vyers? We could use her more than ever," I ask in a desperate tone as I see several more soldiers in need of medical services.

"Negative, sir," Spurs says in a low voice. "The medical wing was lost over two hours ago."

"I'm sure she's just patronizing the enemy to death," Pirez says with the smallest glint of humor as an attempt to hide the sadness in her voice.

"I wouldn't put it past her." I make a half smile to Pirez. "Make those soldiers comfortable," I order, waving my hand towards the wounded.

I stand on a large metal storage container and peer at my remaining soldiers, some with eyes filled with tears, others with the emotionless thousand-yard stare of a man who has seen too much as other's simply clean and reload their weapons to keep themselves distracted. My cervos stand unmoving with the composure of statues. Their training has taught them that there is no time to cry when the enemy is at your doorstep. I stand looking into every face as I begin to speak.

"Soldiers, we've made it this far, we can hold just a little longer," I begin to say as yells come from the soldiers.

"We won't make it! They'll kill us all!" a hysterical Corporal Skyes begins to scream and cry as a few soldiers work to calm her state of distress.

"They just might." I get serious. "But our enemy has clearly underestimated us. We hold the cards now. Their ships are defunct, they are all sick with vacuum exposure and we've forced their command ships to retreat. We outsmarted the biggest fleet ever seen in history; we should be proud! I am proud of every single one of you. You've all looked into the faces of evil and are still here. I used to see you as children that I constantly had to be a parent to but, you know what I see now? I see soldiers of Earth. I see the faces of heroes standing before me. Our fight is over; in seven hours the message will be sent out and help will come. Everyone sit and relax for now, you've all earned it," I finish my speech to a quiet crowd as slowly the cervos begin to stamp their feet. Soon everyone is as I step down from the crate and sit down.

I sit with my mask open, trying to ignore the constant noise of damage reports coming in from my HUD. At this point the enemy have free run of the entire station and are beginning to strip it for parts and electronics. I watch as several soldiers hand out rations taken from the small food cache kept for pilots and engineers in the hangar. I force down the sweet pastry and jerked meat given to me and wash it down with water from a metal canteen. Everyone sits quietly as the occasional echoing thud comes through the thick walls of the hangar from around the station. Each low rumble sends eyes darting towards the doors and forces hands to readied weapons. Each minute passes like an eternity as I ponder why the enemy hasn't dragged their plasma cutter down here to finish us off and soon find myself repeating passages from *The Art of War* in my head. *'If the enemy sees an advantage to be gained and makes no effort to secure it, the soldiers are exhausted.'* I dwell more on the fact that our life support and communications haven't been severed yet and that perhaps the enemy isn't here for us but rather something we have.

"Permission to speak, sir?" the voice of Donovan calls as his question pulls me from my search for insight.

"Go ahead," I say back, looking up and seeing Donovan accompanied by Corporal Chase, an engineer and pilot that works here in the hangar.

"Corporal Chase and I had an idea." He pauses, ensuring he has my attention before he continues. "We could use our five scouting ships and the cervos could hold onto the exteriors and we could ferry them to the main entrance to take the enemy from behind," he says with confidence.

"I expected better from you, Donovan," I say in a cold tone as my eyes burn through his. "First, we have no idea how many more of those monsters are out there. Second, if we open even one of the hangar doors we would literally be letting the enemy shoot us like fish in a barrel. And third—" I stand and yell at the terrible idea as Corporal Chase cuts me off.

"Then at least let us go out there and shoot them, sir! The scanners haven't picked up any ships in the sky in two hours, they're all on the ground, sir. I'm the best pilot on this station, let me do this, sir," he says with his hands behind his back and his chin held high.

"You may be the best pilot on this station, but you're only a drop of water in the ocean of great pilots in this military and even they would think this idea to be too dangerous and risky," I begin to shout at the Corporal Chase as Major Pirez steps between us and looks at me.

"Commander, if I may?" she asks as I huff and grow red in the face but nod in acceptance as she turns to the pair across from me. "If you want the ships to last, you'll need to break two down to reinforce the other three. You both go gather six men and get started, I'll join you soon. Dismissed," she says to them in a calm but commanding tone as I breathe deeply trying to lower my blood pressure. She tightens her ponytail and turns to meet my eyes. "Sorry, Commander, but they need distraction. It will keep them from breaking. I don't plan on opening the doors either, I'm just trying to keep the men sane." My eyes avert hers in a small bout of shame. "Maybe you could use a little too?" she suggests with a caring half smile.

"Thank you, Sasha," I say with a nod as I find my makeshift chair and sit across from Fawkes, beads of sweat pouring from his brow.

A few more hours pass as I sit and drink from my canteen, Fawkes sitting across from me. I pass him the water and watch as he downs the rest. He drops the metal bottle on the ground and looks at me as water trickles down the hairs of his greying beard. He stares into my eyes for a moment before speaking.

"Mind if I ask about Arili?" he asks in a flat tone as his eyes try to find emotion in my face.

"Who told you about Arili?" I ask with perplexity as I haven't mentioned it once to him.

"Your sword," he says as he nods to the blood-crusted sword leaning next to me, its blade etched with my name and that of the planet Arili. "I heard you guys got it bad there."

I stare at the blade and think to myself for a moment before taking a deep breath and speaking.

"I was Field Commander of the nine hundred and fifth armored infantry; three hundred cervos and eight thousand standard soldiers. I was placed in charge of the defense of a province called The Malachite Valley and its sixteen mining communities, a total population of around eight hundred thousand." As I recite my story I can smell the engine fuel, the iron-heavy dust that blew in the wind and I see the shine of the massive sun against the red and grey landscape. "One morning we got a scanner report showing that three northern communities were gone, not just attacked or run off, they were literally wiped off the map. We had no idea what was going on when we got reports of serfs in the north armed with stolen mining equipment. turns out they stole several ship-mounted plasma cutters and overclocked them somehow. The attacks caused a massive sandstorm that became unruly and I called for an all-out evacuation to the closest blast shelter. We evacuated the almost fifty thousand citizens from the city of Rolse when the storm hit with the enemy not far behind. Thirty-seven thousand were still outside the shelter when the exterior sensors picked up the heavy plasma in the air and went into emergency lockdown." I don't break eye contact as I take another deep breath. "I ordered thirty cervos to hold the door up, myself included, and we held the door till every last man woman and child was inside. Three others and myself were last to get out from under the sixty-ton door when my suit malfunctioned and I took the full force of it. It was only three seconds but it was long enough to shatter both shoulder blades, my left collarbone and compress six disks in my upper spine. My suit saved my life." His face is blank of emotion as he watches me speak. "Spent the last two years of the war in a hospital bed, unable to even move my lips to smile when I heard the news of the serf surrender." I finish my story and we both sit there staring at one another for what feels like minutes, his eyes glancing around my face before he speaks.

"I found out from a pay-by-the-hour holo-café, about three hours after my release. At least you got this place for it," he says with a half smirk and a nod of his head.

"Not all they talked it up to be," I say with a huff of humor. "During the war, this place was a fully functioning battle station. By the time I took command it was a recon station with a skeleton crew," I say as I motion for him to look around.

"That's true," he says with a considerate voice as he stands and puts a hand on my shoulder. "But at least this place got you," he says in a humbling tone as he shrugs and slowly walks passed me.

I nod as he walks away and sit there motionless, my eyes the only thing moving as I look over the hangar. A few dozen soldiers have taken to sleeping while others hold watch with guns ready. Others sit in small groups mourning the dead as they bow their heads and recite their names. My eyes travel up and around to the four stories of empty rigs built to hold fighter ships. I think back to one of my first days on the station when the ships were recalled for use elsewhere. I recall how badly I ground my teeth as I watched two hundred fighter class ships fly out of the hangar roof and up to the orbital defense cruiser that was then also reallocated. I grind my teeth now as hard as I did that day as I watch Pirez work with Donovan, Chase and a few other engineers on the only ships we have. They've been working hard and have almost finished reinforcing the hulls of the three remaining ships. As I watch I see her look down at her haptic glove then run over and grab a holo-tab in a hurry and begin to go over something. She reads for a few seconds then darts in my direction. *'Great, what now?'*

"Sir, I hate to be the bearer of—" she begins as I cut her off.

"What's wrong?" I ask, standing before her.

"Sir, we've lost most of our internal systems. Power's been lost on the first floor and door command depends solely on your override. Communications are still operational but it looks like they're trying to hack the command terminals. If they do, they would have complete control of the station. They could be trying to cut the upload link or even open the hangar door," she states in a frightful voice as her hands tremble as she speaks to me.

"I don't think they know about the upload, Sasha," I say with an affirmative tone. "I think they're after our database. If they haven't severed communications then they must be trying to get a signal out, or maybe perform an upload of their own."

"What would pirates want with our database?" she retorts

with uncertainty.

"Shipping routes, personnel rosters, maybe they want our medical knowledge. They might even cut the upload by accident and that means our only option is to stop them here and now; we have no other choice." I nod to her as I turn and stand atop my crate. "I want everybody front and center now!" My shout echoes through the hangar as every soldier stands and hurries to a position in front of me. "It appears our enemy wants something more than our blood." I watch as their eyes glue to my face. "As we speak they are attempting to hack our command consoles. What they seek there, we are unsure of, but we will not let this happen, crew. I am now asking for five volunteers to make a last-ditch charge for the command center," I order as my eyes meet the facemask of every cervo standing before me.

There is silence as everyone begins to look around at each other, their faces speaking volumes as I see the hesitation on many of them. Seconds pass as my remaining cervos all step forward, including Spurs, Fawkes and even Donovan steps up next to them. A shiver goes up my spine as I become so proud of my men for their loyalty. I point to Fawkes and four random others as Donovan steps forward with a sad face.

"Commander? Have I done something wrong? I want to help," he asks, clearly upset at my choice.

"Not at all, Donovan," I say, placing a hand on his shoulder as I loom over him. "If we fail, this place will need a leader, and with that I am promoting you to the rank of Major," I say, looking into his eyes as he cuts in.

"But Pirez is much more suited—" he begins to justify as I put a hand up to stop his rambling.

"Pirez is an engineer, and I hate to admit it but you know the responsibilities of the command center better than any of us.

You'll make a great leader, even Thorne thought so," I say, tearing up at the thought of Adrian in the past tense. "And besides, you're needed for the back-up plan." I wink and smile through the tears rising in my vision as I pull him close and give him a firm gracious handshake. As I let his hand go and we part, the space between us is filled with Major Pirez as she throws her arms around me. "If we fail, open the hangar doors and unleash hell," I whisper to the both of them as she holds on for so long that I have to force her off with the help of Donovan.

I turn to Fawkes and my four other chosen units as we walk towards the sealed door that has the most direct route to central command. The rhythmic beating of hooves echo off the walls as we approach.

"Chime in," I order as we stand there side by side.

"Clause."

"Spurs."

"Howell."

"Gray."

"Fawkes."

My herd calls in over the speakers as I order the door to open with my override key and I look at the upload timer on my HUD: forty-seven minutes remaining.

Chapter 18

One Last Stampede

The door shifts open to a dark hallway with a long ascending staircase to the first floor. We climb step by step slowly to the top. The dull blue glow of the emergency lights is the only thing lighting our path as we walk.

"Gray and Howell, you two are with Clause. I want you to hold back and give cover fire once we engage," I order over the comms. "Fawkes and Spurs, you two are with me; we will take point and engage with melee, understood?" I ask as they each respond affirmative.

We come to the landing in front of the sealed door, the sound of activity on the other side. I activate my override code and order the door to open. It shifts loudly as the metal door slides into the ceiling. The emergency lights flicker above. As I step into the first floor, I see several large groups of savages tearing at the electronics from the walls as others pile the salvage onto small carts. Their faces grow from curiosity to fear as they see three of us looming towards them at great speed. Cover fire opens up from behind us. I draw my pistol in one hand and tighten the grip on my sword in the other as I swing at the closest target; a haggard man in a faded blue bandana drops to his knees as I thrust deep into his chest cavity. I pull my pistol up and drop four more in the distance as Fawkes charges in with his hammer, clearing a group of three with a heavy sideways swing. Another tries to run past and escape but Spurs grabs him by the arm and hurls him back down the hallway. Many flee in screaming terror as we rip through a large portion of their position; others attempt to hold us back but we are unrelenting and give no quarter to any in our path. We move forward as two groups of three, clearing halls as we dash at incredible speeds through the enemy.

I bolt around a corner and instantly feel a spread of bullets across my chest, pushing me back from the concussive force. I dash back into the cover of the corner as my men stand beside me. I peer around quickly and see a small position set up about thirty meters down the hall, a few dozen mongrels are hunkered down with one of our mini-guns.

"They've got a cozy set-up." I say talking to my soldiers. "I want two on the walls, two on the ground and two to hold back and give cover fire." I order, giving hand signals to tell each man his position, each nodding with affirmation. "On my mark," I say as I turn the corner with Spurs at my side.

The mini-gun and firearms of the enemy tear through the dimly lit hallways as we charge them, the bullets sparking off our armor and the metal walls. I get about half way down the hall when I notice this encampment is placed on the threshold of a security door. I smile as I remotely activate it with my override code. I see the confused faces of the enemy as they watch a three-foot-thick metal door descend on them with great speed, crushing several and knocking the mini-gun from its tripod. The small number of enemies remaining on our side of the door smash against it with their weapons in a sad attempt to escape us. Though for them it is too late as the four of us land and tear them apart in seconds; one even tries to surrender but my sword finds his chest before he has a chance to beg. We relieve them of a few grenades and the mini-gun as I command the door to open only a few inches. With the pull of the pins we roll the grenades under the door. A few quaking rambles of fear come from the other side as the grenades detonate, dust and blood coming in from under the thick steel door. After the dust settles I order the door to fully open where we see several pieces of the enemy strewn about. We take no care as we trudge through their remains and continue down the hall.

We arrive outside an entryway into the atrium. From the distance I can see bright fluorescent light shining on the floor from the threshold and can hear commotion in the distance. I approach slowly and see what looks like a feast taking place. Big spotlights have been set up to illuminate the room. My antlers tell me there are trace amounts of fire and cooked meat in the air as I see several bodies, including Thorne's, being butchered and cooked on hot plates in the center of the grand room. At least one hundred of these monsters are gathered around makeshift tables, laughing and cheering as if they had already achieved victory. I step in slowly, unnoticed, only a few feet and see a small generator placed not far from me. I approach it quickly with a heavy hoof. The lights cut out, leaving the room almost pitch black aside from the large hole in the station's main door and the low dull hue of the emergency lights.

"We're not dead yet, fuckers!" I yell at full volume from my speakers as the night vision activates in my suit and I see the frightened faces of my enemy.

They scramble for their weapons as I run for the closest table and flip it with one hand, crushing the three on the other side. My sword slashes and thrusts from my right hand as my left grabs one by the face and clamps down with full force as his skull crushes under the weight. They scatter like cockroaches as they hobble to their feet in confused terror; many rush for the main door but are cut off by Spurs as he locks his boots in place in front of the ten-foot hole and swings a large piece of metal pipe like a bat to keep them at bay. Muzzle bursts flash around the room as the enemy attempts to take control of the situation, not sure where to fire as they hear screams come from all around them. Fawkes stands in the entryway and opens fire with the mini-gun. Pink and red sprays of blood burst out from enemies as he sweeps through their numbers until the gun empties and he engages with his hammer. A malnourished-looking woman charges me with an axe but is shot down a few feet from my reach. I look up and see Clause and the cover team leaping from wall to wall using their hooves to lock in place as they pepper the enemy with rail rifle fire from above. One hundred drops to a dozen in under two minutes as the remainder attempt to flee up the atrium stairs, most throwing their weapons down to dash away from us more easily. With a small group still trailing on the stairs, I brace my legs and leap high into the air almost to the forty-foot-high ceiling as I come down hard on the staircase. A burst of concrete dust blankets my vision as my suit switches to thermal scanners. I see only pieces of bodies through the dust as their heat signatures slowly turn from red to blue. I feel a creak and hear metal bending as the stairs bow and begin to give way. I leap down as the staircase collapses beneath me and land amongst my herd.

"We leap to the second floor and dash for central, understood?" I order to my men as they nod. "Nothing holds us back," I say as I run towards the landing and leap up as I bound through the melted doors to the second floor.

I land in the hallway and turn as my stomach churns inside me and my heart drops. Easily over another hundred enemies now hold our old defensive position in front of the command center. A stretch of hallway one hundred meters long now stands before us and the command center doors; a small intersecting hall sits halfway across the heavy position. I can hear mini-guns warming up as gunfire splashes against my armor and that of my herd. I throw an arm up to protect my faceplate as I charge the enemy. I hurtle myself towards the enemy lines as they open fire, sparks of bullet fire cracking on my suit as I meet them. I plant my foot in front of the first barricade and give it a heavy kick as I activate a pulse blast from my hoof. It sends the concrete back, pulverizing the men ducked behind it. The long barrel of a rifle points at me. As I grab it and bend the metal upward, the man pulls the trigger and his weapon explodes in his hands.

"Clause! Bring down that mini-gun array!" I shout as my team tears through the first twenty meters of the blockade.

"On it, sir!" he shouts back as his team leaps up the walls and darts along them in great strides towards the center position.

The guns spring to life as rapid-fire rounds tear along the walls like an opening zipper, their barrels glowing hot within seconds of firing. All three turrets focus fire on Gray from their tiered position, their bullets taking chips from his armor as he gets only meters away from them. I see a lucky shot hit one of his hooves and unbalance him as he drops to the ground with force. The guns follow his suit and unload on his prone body, not caring if they kill their own, until he stops moving. They cheer as one of my herd dies in front of me but the cheers end quickly when Clause and Howell reach them; the two of them tear the scaffolding apart from the top down in seconds including the mini-gun operators. They disappear below my field of vision as a grenade lands at my feet. I quickly give it a small kick back down the hall when it erupts with a burst of force and shrapnel. My team and I inch meter by meter when Clause calls in over the comm link.

"He's here! He's fucking here!" he screams in sheer terror.

I look up, not seeing my soldiers but over the head of the enemy I can see a massive black glass warpick being raised high. It drops below my sight as I feel the shudder of his pick connect with the floor. Without thinking I brace my legs and leap into the air over the heads of the enemy horde. Twenty meters away I can see Clause and Howell are surrounded and engaging with the black-clad titan. I see Clause attempt to stand as the beast kicks him in the chest and back to the ground with a heavy clang. Howell attempts to take advantage and jumps five meters into the air as the enemy cervo grabs his ankle with amazing reflexes. He swings Howell around, smashing him against a corner that crunches in under his weight and throws him to the ground. He places one of his heavy hooves over Howell's faceplate and activates a powerful magnetic burst from his functional hoof. Howell screams over the comm lines and goes limp as the magnetic burst shatters his faceplate.

I land and collide with the demon, knocking him off balance and causing him to drop his pick as I begin thrusting with my sword looking for a weak point. We exchange blows as he uses his thick forearm as a shield to block my slashes and counters with a heavy punch to the chest that sends me against the wall and to the ground. I look up and see the beast dodge a swing from Clause and grab him by the wrist as he brings his foot to Clause's chest and fires another magnetic burst. Clause's arm tears from the socket as his body is thrust back amongst the rabble of enemies that jump on his body with glee and begin stabbing into the open wound and into his heart.

I stand lunging at him as Fawkes and Spurs land to engage with the titan. He grabs Spurs by the head and tosses him aside as Fawkes moves in. I come down with a heavy swing as Fawkes comes in from behind but the monster grabs my sword by the blade and snaps it in two. He turns, taking the broken half off, and buries it with great force between a small gap in Fawkes' shoulder plate. The blade sinks deep as Fawkes cries over the comms. Spurs rejoins as we continue the fight against this brick wall of a man. Even at three against one, we are no match for him. He kicks Fawkes to the ground as he swings with a heavy gauntlet and hits Spurs in the faceplate, cracks appearing when he connects with the glass visor.

"You should run, Commander! Go! Go get to command! I've got this!" Fawkes yells as he stands to exchange more blows with the savage.

"What the hell are you talking about? He's going to tear you apart!" I bark back.

"Remember that shotgun blast I took?" He pauses as he swings. "Well, it blew the cooling cap off my fusion core," he says between grunts and throwing punches.

"But without the coolant injection, your core will go atomic if you eject!" I yell, trying to rationalize with him as I pommel the rib cage of an enemy that thought he could sneak up on me.

"Yeah, but he doesn't know that! You should run, Commander. Go get your kids home safe," he says with a bolstered voice as his fist connects with the chin of the black titan; it does nothing but enrage the beast even more.

"Run for command!" I yell to Spurs as we turn and dash. "You fought well, Commander Fawkes. It's been a pleasure," I say as I activate my hooves readying for a leap.

"Just don't let them make a statue of me, all right?" He chuckles with gallows humor.

I make it about twenty meters before I hear the explosion.

The back of my suit grows searing hot as my hooves fail and I'm washed in a bright light. I feel Spurs' suit push against the back of mine when everything suddenly goes black. I'm sideways as I open my eyes and see the devastation in the room. Spurs lies dead beside me in a heap of scorched metal. My mask is smashed and my suit sparks and seizes in some areas. The magnetic generators in my hooves are melted as I try to move my legs but find it harder than ever to move them. I shift as best I can and see the hall behind me and see it littered in dust and corpses. A large hole has been gouged into the roof and the hallways are bowing and drip with melted steel. Amongst the heaps I can see parts of Fawkes' armor and spot pieces that were once the black-clad titan. I shift more, trying to stand, but lose all my strength and collapse in my suit, my eyes glaring at the ceiling. I stare into the white scorched ceilings tiles as my body fills with a wash of pain. My arms hurt more right now than they did when I first broke them. I lie there trying to stay conscious when suddenly an air duct up near the ceiling begins to rattle as I watch it shudder and shake.

"Now they're in the fucking vents?" I question and scream out loud. "Just fucking do it, you animals! You've come this far, so just fucking finish it!" I scream as I lay there in my dying suit, laughing with hysteria. The vent pops open and falls with a clamorous thud. As I peer at the dark open vent, my heart drops at what I see slowly creep from the metal hole: a small shiny green droid hovers out and descends towards me.

"I told you they were of better use to me, Commander," the robotic voice of Dr. Vyers screeches out over the droid's crackling speakers. It gets close and casts its green scanning light over me and my suit.

"Dr. Vyers? Claire, you're alive?" I try to move but my arms won't even respond and I wince in pain.

"Yes, Commander. I'm safe, I assure you. The medical wing has many nooks and crannies." I watch as droid finishes its scans. "I'd like to apologize. I couldn't help but keep one of my droids." As she speaks a part of the droid's belly slides open and a metal claw with a syringe inches out towards me.

"I should have listened to you, Claire. I—" I attempt to apologize but she cuts me off.

"Well then listen to me now, Commander," she says calmly as her droid injects me with a shot of stimulant. "Go finish this. Go show these monsters what a real soldier of Earth can do," she says as I feel a rush of euphoria come with the injection, my eyes widening and my pain subsiding.

"Doctor's orders," I say and slowly stand in my suit and begin to wobble towards the ten steps to the command center.

With each step I try to work past the fading pain as I try to go to my happy place on Arili, though when I close my eyes this time I don't see Arili. This time I see the faces of Majors Thorne and Pirez at morning briefing. I see Donovan and Skyes at their posts, I see the smiling faces of Mackie and Welsh, I remember the drinks and stories I once shared with each of my cervos. Arili isn't my happy place anymore, it's Whitman Station, and I'm not about to let anyone else take that from me. Each step is easier as I come to the realization that this is my home, this is where I stood in the face of monsters with the bravest souls I've ever met. With the face of every man and woman of this crew flashing through my mind, I climb the last step outside the command center. I see a makeshift barricade placed before me and the molten hole to my objective. I shove it out of the way with a heavy push as I enter my command center and step in. I see at least three dozen savages rushing around the terminals and a large portable satellite sitting in the middle of the room. Large bundles of cables run from the satellite to many of the command terminals as these enemies work the keyboards in a hurried manner. The room goes dead quiet as they see me walk in and stand in the threshold. I see each of these mongrels look at me as I sneer my eyes and part my lips.

"Officer on deck," I say in an angry bravado.

Chapter 19

The Face of My Enemy

I charge towards the closest enemy as he aims his gun at me. I stop the round with an open palm from my hand and backhand him so hard I see the back of the man's head. Several rounds come bursting at me from the terminals as I grab a sheet of metal from in front of me and hold it like a shield. I dash towards them as I barrel into their position, pinning one against the wall and throwing blood out the sides of the shield. I turn to advancing savages and throw the sheet metal like a discus as a corner finds the chest of an enemy. He shrieks briefly before falling lifeless to the ground. Two others move close with metal clubs. I grab one club mid-swing and take it in my hand, smashing the head of its previous owner. I follow through and bend the knee of the other inward with a heavy smack; he drops and screams as I bring my knee to my chest and drop my foot on his face. Two more open fire across the room as I duck behind a set of terminals. I feel a shot ricochet off the temple of my helmet, just missing my open face. From over the terminals a mongrel leaps onto my chest with a large knife. I disarm him by crushing his hand with mine as I grab him by the throat and stand pointing him towards his companions. They open fire as I run in their direction, putting holes in their teammate. I whip the dead man at the enemy on the left and charge the one on the right. I stamp my left foot over his right foot and punch as hard as I can; he falls directly back with a small burst of blood as his head connects with the floor.

I turn and see the tip of a homemade spear thrust past my face and slice my cheek. I feel warm blood flow down into the neck of my suit. I reach out and grab the shaft of the spear and pull, causing the wielder to overextend, putting the end of the spear over his stomach. I push down with a quick jerk and put the butt-end through him to the ground. I unsheathe the spear from its human scabbard and begin thrusting at the incoming enemies. I plunge the spear through the stomach of a charging enemy and pull to the left as I open him from front to back as his innards spill from the wound. He drops as the spear slashes across the face of the savage beside him, chunks of hair and meat resting on the tip and the shaft of the blood-soaked spear. I sweep the legs of the next charging mongrel as bullets spark across my chest plate. I look up and see a man firing a homemade automatic rifle at me from across the room. I pull my arm back and launch the spear towards him. As it pins him to the wall through his chest, his arms go limp and his head sags as his gun drops to the ground. A companion of his attempts to grab his rifle from the ground as I dash towards him crushing the enemy on the ground in front of me. As I collide into him and smash him into the wall, I can feel the reverberations of his bones breaking through my suit. I pull my spear free and turn with my back to the wall, surveying the remaining enemies.

Six more fall to my spear as I see several make for the door and retreat, leaving only seven behind that begin to circle me. I snap the spear in two across my leg and wield both pieces. They scream as they charge me as one. I block the first one with my left hand and thrust with my right into their abdomen as I horse-kick backward, sending one barreling into the wall, his limp body dead before impact. Another takes an elbow to the jaw as I smack one in the neck with my makeshift club, leaving him to suffocate as he clutches his neck. I impale another on my spear as I roar. I see only red as I thrust the spear into the eye socket of an enemy. I pull back and throw the spear into one more as the last one stands with a broken jaw and bloody nose. I hold up the broken shaft and charge him with all the might I have left. I barrel into him as the shaft slides through his chest with ease; I keep charging until I impale him on the satellite. The entire console begins to spark as the impaled savage shakes and convulses from the electricity flowing through him. I rear my leg up and kick as hard as I can into the dish. It wobbles and sparks as it bends and teeters at its base then snaps with a satisfying sound as it smashes against the ground.

I look around for anyone else but only see corpses. I hear the warning signs of my suit failing and sit down against a block of terminals. I take several deep breaths and wait for anyone else as I breathe a sigh of relief and close my eyes, letting my head fall back against the steel. Suddenly I hear a voice in the room and I open my eyes to the soft blue glow of the holo-comms system. I see me standing there only a few feet away in my officer's uniform. My eyes wander up to find my own staring blankly in its soft blue radiance.

"This is Commander Haves of station P4X-1711, otherwise known as Whitman Station here in the Epsilon Eridani system. This is an all emergency alert. Our station is under attack by a large unknown force. A fleet larger than Bilemy has emerged from the asteroid belt around our system and is descending upon us as we speak. Attached to this message are sonar and short-range scanner readings along with other data we have collected thus far. We don't know if we can hold out till this message arrives to you, but we will do our best. All for Earth, thank you."

I watch my holographic self-speak as the message ends and the blue hum fades away in a blip. I smile knowing the message got out and close my eyes again.

"Commander Duncan Haves," a deep loamy voice bellows out as my eyes open to a different blue figure standing before me. His dark eyes resting beneath a rigid brow stare blankly yet pierce through me as I watch him.

"Who are you?" I ask as I eye the figure's thick white beard and bald head covered in scars, his clothes looking like that of a tattered officer's uniform.

"I would like to thank you for the skirmish. It was enlightening to say the least," he says with a cracked smile and pompous voice.

"I'd say we won from the looks of it: we took your fleet." I smirk as I watch this figure's perfect posture.

"You simply defeated some pirates, but I learned far more than you won today, Duncan," he retorts with a low bellow. "I see you took my pet today. She was very expensive to make but now I can make more, thanks to you." He smiles as his clasped hands rub each other. "I wonder what we could learn elsewhere, perhaps Boise? The Rock? Laramie? You see, Commander, we can be anywhere we want and soon we will be all you find. It's been a pleasure, Commander," he says with a chuckle as his holograph flickers then disappears before my eyes.

My mind whirls at this news. *That titan was a woman? Who is this guy? Why was he in a uniform? Why so formal for a leader of pirates?* My mind races and my heart drops when it clicks as to who that was.

"That was Admiral Samuel Kist," I mutter as I lean against the wall in disbelief and pull the scorched book of the Cordoba out of the storage compartment on my suit and see the younger version of the man I just saw.

My eyes grow heavy and my vision darkens as I breathe deeply from inside my wrecked suit. *'When did I last sleep?'* I think to myself as the toll I've taken to my body catches up with me. I lie with my eyes closed as a familiar low rumble shakes the command center. *'The hangar?'* My eyes widen as I strain with all my might to rise and run to Pirez to cancel the order. I teeter on my knees and fall flat on my back, seeing I've lost my chance as I see the three reinforced scouting ships fly across the observation window in the ceiling and as they pass I see the exterior of each ship has the remainder of the herd clinging to them. My view of them is brief but the ripple of distant explosions and gunfire can be heard echoing down the now quiet halls of Whitman Station. I lie there with a smile on my face as my eyes close from exhaustion. I hear footsteps in the distance but can't stay awake long enough to know if it's friend or foe.

Chapter 20

The Adelaide

I stand motionless in my steam shower as I recall over and over what happened seven days ago, my eyes staring blankly at the white tile walls of the stall as I lose myself to my thoughts. I should be proud of our victory yet all I feel is anger; anger at the lack of provided personnel, the negligence of our leaders leaving us with outdated equipment, and especially the secrets that lead to all of this. *'I could have saved more,'* I shout in my head as I swing at the tiled walls with a heavy fist. *'They didn't deserve this!'* I clench my jaw as another swing connects with the white porcelain. I'm about to swing again when my haptic glove pings with a comms request. I step from my shower and gather my glove from the edge of the bed and accept the call.

"This is Haves," I bark into the microphone.

"Commander, Admiral Granne will be arriving with his fleet in one hour and has requested you be there in the hangar for his landing approach," Donovan says through the speaker in my glove.

"Thank you, Major, I'll see you down there. Haves out," I say in a forced bravado.

'You can do this,' I repeat to myself as I stand before the mirror in a towel, my body riddled with dark and tender bruises. I glare into my brown eyes still dull with exhaustion as my hand finds the nine stitches that now cross my cheek from the spear

thrust. *'They're the heroes, dammit, why give me all the glory?'* My fingers run down my salt and pepper beard as I contemplate the events of the past week: the gathering of the dead for burial, the wailing cries of our less constitute soldiers, and the mountains of redundant paperwork that followed. *'Loyal soldiers died and all they care about is combat reports. Waste of fucking time if you ask me, because that bastard is still out there.'* I turn and shift my gaze to my dress uniform that lies folded on my bed. Every muscle in me aches as I struggle to clothe myself. My eyes lock onto the fragment of Fawkes' suit and Thorne's helmet that both now sit on my desk; I draw strength from their sacrifice as I finish with the final buttons of my uniform. I walk slowly to the door and turn back, peering over my shoulder to scan my room. *'Bed. Check. Shower. Check. Shave?'* My hand rubs the hairs of my chin. *'Not anymore.'*

The halls of the station are in disrepair as I work my way through to the hangar. Lighting dangles from its cords, empty holes once housing terminals now dot the walls alongside the bloodstains and bullet holes. *'The walls will never be white again.'* I ordered the officer's wing be last on clean-up duty to ensure everyone else was taken care of first; the bodies are the only thing removed thus far. The wreckage of the ships will take years to clean up. Almost half the fleet was shot down and the rest lie abandoned around the outskirts of the station. We've learned much about our new enemy from searching the wreckage: based on what writings and scribblings we found inside the junkers, they spoke a mutated form of English. The inner hulls of their ships were filled with pictographs and graffiti. Many of these images depicted a man in a ray of light like a savior. We could only assume it is a depiction of Admiral Kist. Though we scoured the ships for any information as to where they got all the fuel for their fleet, or how they managed to live inside the asteroid belt, we found nothing that brought insight to that. *'I imagine all that information is on the Cordoba.'* I walk the northern stairwell down the three levels to engineering, passing the bent bars and hoof-prints left imbedded in the concrete by Fawkes and I. Walking past the wall of scrapped rail gun terminals I don't see a single person until I arrive outside the engineering command center.

"Commander on deck!" Major Donovan yells from his position next to Major Pirez as the seven technicians in the room come to attention.

"At ease," I order as I step in, taking command of the room. "Turn that off," I order again as I see three technicians watching yet another news story about the attack on a terminal screen. News of the attack has been plastered everywhere; I can't turn on a news station without seeing something about Whitman Station. I ordered everyone to keep quiet about the event but it seems someone got a hold of some video fragments that we had sent to High Command and leaked them to the press. The face of Admiral Kist and a few videos clips of the black titan are the main focus of many of these news reports. Documentaries about the Cordoba have been playing almost non-stop across most channels. I walk past the technicians as their screens turn off and approach Donovan and Pirez, both of them also clad in their dress uniform. "How are repairs going?" I ask Pirez.

"Things are slow going, sir. The station is currently running at thirty-six percent efficiency. We've re-established a majority of our internal systems but without new parts we won't last another week," she says as her eyes dance across her holo-tab trying to find solutions.

"New crew and parts are only an hour away so try not to worry so much." I smile with assuredness as I turn to Donovan.

"Any more sightings of stragglers?" I ask him.

"Last one was two days ago, sir, haven't heard a peep since. There aren't many places to hide out there. If they're out there we will find them, sir." He nods and smiles at his and the remaining herd's success in flushing out the remnants of our enemy.

"Excellent. Continue your lookout routines and have the pilots carry on with their aerial scouting," I order as I offer a nod to the both of them. "We should head for the hangar; the Admiral has asked us to be present when he arrives." I motion as I walk past them towards the hangar, both following closely behind.

I stride into the hangar with my Majors in tow. It's active with several engineers standing amongst command consoles and clearing the landing pads for the coming influx of ships. I climb the platform to the console station and stand behind the technicians, their hands working the terminal screens with extreme precision. Major Pirez takes command amongst them and begins final checks for the fleet's approach.

"The Adelaide is approaching the atmosphere, sir," she says, looking up from her console, her finger circling the activation button.

"Open the hangar doors, Major," I order as my head tilts back to see the two massive steel shutters that separate us from the outside.

She activates the opening sequence as the large hydraulic arms spring to life and pull down and begin to separate the seventeen-foot-thick steel slabs that begin to slide into the walls beside them. The eternal sunlight washes the hangar in a brilliant glow as I look up at the bright sky, clear blue until a single dark figure looms high in the distance. It grows darker as it gets closer, its outline showing it to be easily three times the size of the Cordoba. The Adelaide is the flagship of the *Eridani Armada*, built to house its entire fleet within itself and over fifteen thousand personnel and their families. Its purpose is the defense and monitoring of all habitable stations located beyond the outer asteroid belt of the solar system, which spans the circumference of billions of kilometers and over one hundred stations and colonies call it home.

Everyone in the hangar watches with dropped jaws as the belly of the colossal ship begins to open like the mouth of a massive dragon, the large square belly folding open as dozens of ships begin to descend towards us. Landing requests begin flowing in across the monitors as Pirez and her technicians guide each ship down onto a landing pad. A larger command vessel is visible amongst the fleet of fighters and transports as well as the officer's transport that we sent off. The Eridani fleet picked them up two days ago. I nod for Donovan to follow me as I approach the central landing pad, the command ship's thrusters whirling down as its forward hatch slides open and two figure step out amongst an honor guard of six white-clad cervo units in Mark3 C-suits. The Mark3 suits are beautiful to look at, almost a foot taller than the Mark2 and with a beautiful white enamel baked over the black glass steel; it even looks like the arms now have built in rail rifles. Of the two figures walking between them, the first is almost a foot taller than me with incredibly dark hair. His face, though, is far more aged with years of combat. Though he is my superior in this sector, this is my first time meeting the Admiral face to face. *'Dyed hair? Really? He can't be much older than me.'* I have seen plenty of pictures of Admiral Granne and held several video conversations but wasn't expecting such a presence from the man. He's easily seven feet tall and quite stout with a large burly chest. Walking beside the large and well-dressed Admiral is a man in a grey and silver uniform that I'm not familiar with. Large glasses sit behind a long mess of dirty blonde bangs with a strange leather-bound book clutched in his arms.

"Admiral Granne, welcome to Whitman Station. It's good to finally meet you in person, sir." I salute as I address my superior.

"Commander Haves." He salutes back and gestures to the man in the silver uniform next to him. "This is EIC Inquisitor Sands. He will be joining us during this investigation." *'An actual inquisitor?'*

"A pleasure to meet you, Inquisitor Sands." I salute. "This is Major Donovan; he is my second in command here on the station." Donovan salutes but is brushed off as the Admiral begins to speak.

"Major Donovan, you will remain here until you are called upon. As for you, Commander Haves, please guide us to the briefing room." He motions with sudden disdain on his face as Donovan gets an awkward look on his face.

"The briefing room was scrapped by the enemy; we've been using an office in engineering," I say with clear confusion on my voice.

"So be it." He huffs. "Take us there then," he demands as he swats his hands in a *move it* fashion.

"Admiral, with all due respect, isn't this supposed to be a decoration ceremony?" I ask plainly as his eyes sneer at me.

"No," he says bluntly. "This is an investigation."

"Am I under arrest?" I ask with a slight touch of sarcasm.

"Not yet," he says without even looking at me.

"Of course, uhhh… Right this way, Admiral," I say with a stammer and turn, leading him and the Inquisitor from the hangar as I take a quick moment to look at my majors. Their faces are pale with clear confusion as I give a shrug of uncertainty to them and exit the hangar.

Chapter 21

Sudden Accusations

My heart pounds like I just ran a marathon as I open the door to the repurposed office and step in. A large portable folding table sits in the middle of the small room amongst storage crates lined against the wall with four simple metal folding chairs placed around it. The Admiral motions for me to sit across from him and the Inquisitor as they each take a seat with their back to the door. I sit across from them and place my hands and elbows on the table to ease the weight on my shoulders and sit there quietly for a few moments as the Inquisitor prepares himself. The awkward man in the silver and grey uniform does something I find incredibly peculiar: he places the large leather-bound book open on the table and pulls a large fountain pen out. As I sit with a notched eyebrow and watch him the Admiral takes notice and begins to speak.

"Books are harder to hack these days," he says, knowing that's what I found so strange, as a moment later the Inquisitor simply looks to Granne and nods. "Let us begin then. Commander, can you state your name for the record please?" he orders from across the table.

"Of course. Commander Duncan Phillip Haves, identification number CC-MST1534," I say in an unshaken bravado. *'I've got nothing to hide,'* I remind myself as the Inquisitor writes at an impressive speed.

"Thank you, Commander," he states as he pulls a cigarette from an ornate silver case and lights it, taking a long drag as the embers burn and the room fills with the smell of tobacco. "And how long have you been in command of Whitman Station?" he asks as he flicks his ashes on the floor.

"Just over eight years, sir," I say in my well-practiced tone for speaking with superiors.

"And after eight years, it would be safe to say that you know your crew?" he asks with his eyebrows high as smoke flows from his nose like an angry dragon.

"Of course, through and through, sir. I trust every single one of them," I say with truthful confidence. *'I can tell where this is going,'* I think to myself as I prepare for a thorough grilling.

"Then tell me about your chief of medicine, Commander," he demands as his eyes glare at me through the wisps of smoke dancing around his head.

"Dr. Vyers?" I ask rhetorically. "She's been here over thirty years and has tended to every single member of personnel in one way or another," I answer with honesty.

"So you're saying it would be unlikely for her to sell information?" he asks as his eyes narrow as they peer into mine.

"Impossible." I shake my head. "If not for her, this place would be gone; her droid saved my life, sir," I say in a professional tone.

"A droid that, according to your report, had been ordered to be placed on the eastern side of the facility, yes?" he returns with a small condescending smile.

"Under section seven of the standard operating handbook, a soldier may deny an unjust order from their superior, sir," I say as I make the same smile back at him.

"She is a doctor, not a soldier," he says as smoke flows from his mouth.

"She took the same oath we did, sir. I think that applies to her as well," I say logically as I lean back slightly in my chair.

We all sit there quietly for several seconds as Granne crushes the butt of his smoke out on the table and I take a moment to glance at the Inquisitor who hasn't even looked up once since we started talking. His pen simply dances across the page of his book as he transcribes our conversation.

"So then answer me this, Haves. Why would Dr. Vyers requisition all the information on the skeletal system of a cervo unit? That is highly classified information and has now been stolen by these unknown enemies," he asks, barely looking at me as he lights another smoke and inhales deeply from it.

"During the war this station was housing over sixty members of medical staff and several of them were specialized in cervo anatomy, but when the war ended Dr. Vyers was left alone to doctor the entire crew," I say as I make solid eye contact with the Admiral. "Cervo units get injured, Admiral, and Dr. Vyers needed that information to better asses any injuries and prescribe proper medications. Access to this information was approved and sanctioned by High Command on Earth and had been password protected and encrypted to ensure that even if it was stolen, it would be unreadable, sir. Even if they have it, they most likely can't read it," I say as I take a long and deep breath as the Admiral continues smoking and the Inquisitor simply writes in his book, still not once having looked up at either of us. *'Are all Inquisitors like this? Is he just a glorified scribe or something?'* I ponder as I glance at the small, frail-looking man.

"And where is Dr. Vyers now, Commander?" he asks as he exhales a puff of smoke in my direction.

"She is in the medical wing tending to the wounded," I reply with an obvious tone.

"Ah yes, the medical wing that was swarmed with enemy combatants, and yet she survived. You didn't think to question that, Commander?" he asks with sarcasm as I can tell he is trying to catch me in some lie, a tactic I use myself quite often.

"I did actually, Admiral. She showed me the vent she crawled into behind one of her pieces of medical equipment. With her holo-pad she was able to keep an eye on the situation until the enemy started severing our internal systems. That's when she sent her droid to look for me." I lock eyes with the Admiral. "She is the reason we are all here now, sir."

"Do you like your position here, Commander?" he asks nonchalantly between drags of his smoke, acting like he hadn't heard anything I just said.

"I've learned to like it, Admiral," I say reluctantly as I shift in my seat. *'Not like I had much of a choice.'*

"Is that why you've requested seven transfers over the years? Sounds to me like you would love to get off this moon," he says in an accusing tone as his eyes watch my body for a reaction. "Perhaps by any means necessary?" His eyes narrowing as he questions my loyalty.

"I would never betray my fellow humans, Admiral. As I said, I took the same oath you did," I say with slight anger as my hands clench and my knuckles turn white.

"So then explain how you knew the inner workings of a ship that was lost over forty years ago, Commander," he demands as he leans forward with his elbows on the table, smirking as though this is his big moment to catch me in a lie.

"There are at least seven books published discussing the journey of the Cordoba. I enjoy history and own one of those very books, Admiral. If I was working for the enemy, why would I blow a hole through their flagship? If anything, my love of history helped us win this, sir," I question back as I lean in my chair with my arms folded. *'This is fucking ridiculous.'*

"In your report you stated that Admiral Samuel Kist spoke to you over the holo-comms system, correct?" he replies back, avoiding my question.

"He did. I also attached that footage to my report and High Command confirmed through face recognition software that it was indeed him," I answer with increasing impatience of this ridiculous investigation.

"Yes, I saw the footage and you're correct, facial recognition did prove it to be him. So tell me why the two of you were on a first name basis?" he asks with a smug tone and squinting eyes. *'Are you fucking serious?'*

"We weren't, Admiral. It's clear on the footage that I ask him who he is. His knowing my name was most likely due to the fact that he just stole our entire database, which includes the names of every soldier and technician here on the station," I say with confidence.

"Then tell me why you approved the upload sequence!" he demands and yells as he slams his hand on the table, causing me to shudder at the sudden act and catching me off guard.

"The order came from High Command, Admiral. So go ask them why they ordered me to go through with it!" I yell back defending myself.

"Excuse me?" the higher-pitched voice of Inquisitor Sands butts in, silencing the Admiral before he can yell again. "Commander Haves, we have it on record with Commander Cairn at Laramie Station that you gave official approval for the upload," he says plainly as he flips backward through his book and finds the entry and motions for the Admiral to be quiet, the

Admiral sitting back down in disdain but following the order reluctantly.

"Look, I did give the approval for the upload, but only after Commander Cairn had informed me that High Command demanded I follow through with it," I say to the young and scruffy haired Inquisitor.

"Why wasn't this information in your report, Commander?" he asks as he tilts his head inquisitively as if he just received an epiphany.

"I didn't think I had to mention it as I thought it was orders you were already aware of," I say with sincerity seeing these two across from me playing the worst game of good-cop/bad-cop I've ever seen.

"Can you prove this, Commander?" he asks, looking at me as his pen continues to write our conversation without even looking at the page.

"Actually, yes, I can. We record every transmission that comes in through the holo-comms. That's how we obtained the footage of Kist. Isn't it standard protocol to record all transmissions?" I say with a victorious half smile as I look at the Admiral.

"Yes, it is, and I would very much like to see this footage, as according to Commander Cairn at Laramie station, his conversation with you was scrambled due to signal loss." He ponders for a second, his pen still writing as he thinks to himself. "Admiral, if you would be so kind?" He looks to the Admiral who rolls his eyes and then pulls out a holo-tab and accesses the recording.

We sit and watch the entire conversation between Commander Cairn and myself. The eyes of both the Admiral Granne and Inquisitor Sands go wide as the footage comes to an end. They both look at each other as the Inquisitor nods to the Admiral as Granne sits back in a huff and pulls his haptic glove to his face.

"Adelaide, this is Admiral Granne. Establish a link with Commander Cairn at Laramie Station immediately," he orders into his glove as we sit there in silence for several moments that feel like an eternity. More time passes as the Admiral grows restless and pulls his glove to his face again. "Adelaide, report," he orders, clearly impatient as a voice comes through over the speaker.

"Admiral, we have a link with Laramie but Major York says that Commander Cairn is unavailable," the voice says with clear anxiety.

"Unavailable? I've put the entire Oregon Trail on lockdown, he should be there," he questions back to his ship as his eyes dance in worry to Sands and myself.

"Negative, sir. Major York at Laramie claims he took the fleet and left on your orders, Admiral," the disembodied voice says back with hesitation.

"I gave no such orders! Put me through to Major York now!" he shouts into his glove as I watch his face grow deep red as the Inquisitor stands motioning for the Admiral to be silent and brings his haptic glove to his mouth.

"Adelaide, this is Inquisitor Sands. Inform the fleet to offload all remaining supplies and reinforcement crew and prepare for take-off. We are done here," he orders as the Admiral stands with anger and haste. *'An Inquisitor outranks an Admiral?'*

"Now hold on, Sands, we don't know for certain that Cairn is responsible," Granne barks as his face grows red with anger.

"That's Inquisitor Sands, Admiral," the small man says with

gusto to Granne. "You were ready to hang every member of personnel on this station for treason. Now that your protégé is accused you want to deal in certainties? Well, here's some certainties I'm coming to. Commander Cairn couldn't provide us with the evidence we see here, and now he has taken off with the entire Laramie fleet against your orders. I'm leading this investigation, Admiral, and if you like to defend accused turncoats then by all means you will hang with them too. Until then I can put an order through to have the Solstice fleet come and relieve you of command until this situation is solved. Is that what you'd like, Admiral?" the small Inquisitor yells to the large Admiral in a strange depiction of David and Goliath. *'Damn, I like this guy.'*

"No need, I understand, Inquisitor Sands," the Admiral says reluctantly as he averts his eyes from the Inquisitor in shame.

"Thank you for your cooperation, Admiral," he says quietly as he turns back to me. "Commander, I'd like to thank you and your staff for your bravery and service to the human race and to High Command. This portion of my investigation is over and you are free to go," he says calmly as he closes his book and stands, ushering for the Admiral to follow him who does so begrudgingly.

"Just like that?" I ask as I stand slowly.

"Indeed," is all he says as he gathers his book and walks to the door with the Admiral, turning just as he is about to exit. "If the assumptions we've come to on Commander Cairn turn out to be true, there will be an opening for the command position of Laramie Station. Shall I approve your transfer request if this is the case? The human race deserves more men like you, Commander Haves," he asks as he stands in the threshold and makes eye contact through his thick glasses.

"Transfer? No offense, Inquisitor, but why the hell would I want to leave this position?" I say bluntly and scoff at the thought.

The End